FRANCESCA CATLOW loves to travel. Born and raised in the heart of Suffolk, Catlow has travelled extensively in Europe with her French husband and, more recently, their two young children. Of all the places she's been it is the Greek islands that have captured her heart. She visits as often as family commitments allow. The Little Blue Door was Catlow's first novel – written during the lockdown of 2020 while feeding her baby in the early hours.

To stay up to date please visit www.francescacatlow.co.uk.

T: @francescacatlow
F: @francescacatlowofficial
I: @francescacatlowofficial

For trigger warnings visit:
francescacatlow.co.uk/trigger-warnings/

The *Little Blue Door Series* in order:
Book 1: The Little Blue Door (2021)
Book 2: Behind The Olive Trees (2022)
Book 3: Chasing Greek Dreams (2023)

The
Little
Blue
Door

FRANCESCA CATLOW

Gaia
Fenrir

Published in 2021 by SilverWood Books
Second edition published by Gaia & Fenrir in 2021

ISBN 978-1-91520-800-2 (paperback)
ISBN 978-1-91520-801-9 (ebook)

British Library Cataloguing in Publication Data
A CIP catalogue record for this book is
available from the British Library

I dedicate this book to my husband and my mum and dad. Without your endless time and support this would not have been possible. I would also like to dedicate this book to Corfu. Its memory filled my dreams and helped me to get through the 2020 lockdown.

I would like to acknowledge Lesley. Thank you for your help, both on holidays and on the book. www.corfuselections.com

Thank you to San Stefano Travel and Manthos Taverna for your support and inspiration.
https://san-stefano.gr

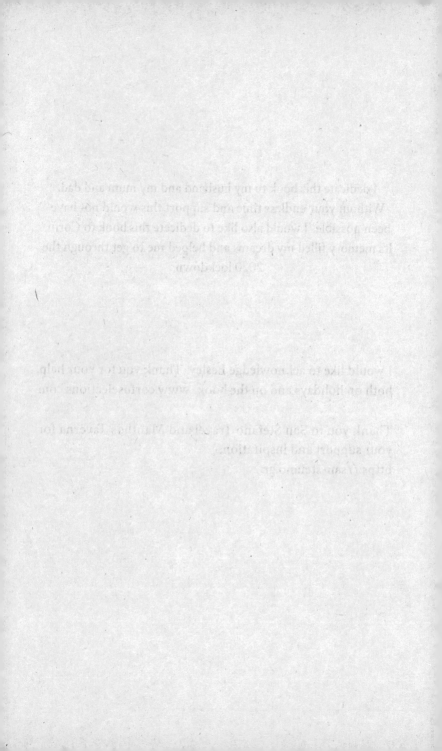

Chapter 1

The sound shook through me – the thrust of air then the anxiety. It made me feel claustrophobic. I'd been all right up until that point. Then the wind decided to blow my hair across my face, leaving some in my mouth. Hair muddled with the taste of jet fuel. I remember instantly wanting to gag.

My heels wobbled underneath me as I did my best to walk steadily. I wasn't a nervous flyer or anything like that. I'd just never flown alone before. I must have been mad to be strolling along in my white heels. I had always liked the old-fashioned idea of dressing up to travel. Bit of a joke, really. I was likely the only person wearing stilettos across the runway to climb up into a plane that day.

The clamber to find the right seat hadn't changed much at the tail end of a pandemic. Social distancing was almost a thing of the past, but many were still wearing morbid-looking face masks, as though half the passengers were off to perform surgeries. The masks were still on. After removing the hair from my mouth, mine was back on too. It was black with a small butterfly motif, my small ray of hope.

I sat down. I don't remember the seat number, only it was on the right. I hadn't even been on public transport for well over a year. I could feel myself twitch and hold my breath with each person who brushed my skin. Unfortunately, I'd been placed between the cliché crying baby and the guy with long legs and pointy elbows. My usual level of luck. In one sly move, I managed to grab the inflight magazine for distraction. I was pretending to flick through it when I noticed her stare. I felt the warm points of someone's eyes lingering far too long on my skin. It made me uncomfortable before I truly knew why, before I knew she was watching me. Then I could see her above the seats, two rows ahead, across to the left. She was shifting about, sometimes eyes between the seats then looking right over the top of them. She didn't look away from me. Even children normally have the common decency to look away when you look back at them, and she wasn't a small child. She must have been around twelve. She was beautifully tanned, with bright green eyes and long dark hair. I sent her a quick smile with the corners of my eyes as she bobbed above her seat, then returned my focus blankly to the magazine.

The girl only stopped observing me when the seat belt sign came on and we all mindlessly watched the flight attendants point to the exits. She unnerved me, the girl. I don't know why, but she did. She felt too young to be so calm and too old not to know better than to stare. Luckily the rest of the flight came and went pretty uneventfully, other than my being dribbled on by the sleeping baby.

My shoes were squeaking during the short walk from passport control to baggage claim. Perhaps it was because my feet had swollen a little on the aeroplane, or maybe it was the silky flooring. Either way, I was a walking music box that had gone out of tune. All I needed was someone to tell me my skirt was tucked into my knickers and I'd tick all the boxes of embarrassing. At least I could blame my flushed cheeks on the heat. In the small airport on Corfu there wasn't the mixture of attire found at Stansted, where people were going to various types of destinations. I really was the only person not in flip- flops, sliders or sandals. Each step seemed to result in yet another head snapping around to see what the problem was: only me.

I lugged my case off the belt and marched in a bid to escape from my own noise. One hand was tugging at the bag while the other thumbed through my emails to dissolve myself into my phone. I turned a sharp right out of baggage claim, and then it hit me. Or rather, *he* hit me. Like whack-a-mole gone wrong, popping up at the hammer. There was no way I could anticipate that someone would rear up in front of me just as I turned that corner. I let out a little involuntary screech. After a year of social distancing, his touch hit me like a cold shower. It sent a wave of goosebumps from the epicentre. I nearly lost my phone in the process. Okay, it's perfectly plausible that he may have been adjusting a shoe or picking up something he'd dropped, and I may have been too distracted by my phone. It still seems rather ludicrous to me – what a stupid place to stop. Either which way, he must have been the only person who hadn't heard my squeak coming from a distance. This slightly painful encounter left a hot patch on my arm from his hard head. Then I noticed her, again.

'*Yassas*.' She looked right at me and spoke her Greek greeting in my direction, as though she knew me.

3

'Hi…and ouch.' That's when I really looked at him. He was tall, maybe six foot four, with a tan to match the girl's, and eyes just as green. Like dark seaweed washed up on golden sands.

'I'm so sorry. I didn't see you there!' He started brushing me down as though I were a child, big hands sweeping my sore, naked arm.

'My name's Gaia.' She spoke coolly, smiling, ignoring the man, ignoring the situation, just looking around him at me.

'The Greek mother of all life?' I retorted, and couldn't help my tone, or my face. The tone and my expression just slipped out of me and I couldn't catch them. A broad smile spread across her mask-free lips.

'Something like that,' she said. I was still being patted down, but I didn't notice much.

'I'm so sorry,' the man kept mumbling over and over again.

'That's okay. Don't worry about it!'

I did my best to hurry away from the beautiful pair, yanking my case around a flimsy barrier, nearly taking it with me. Only a few steps to the exit. I didn't need confusing thoughts in my mind, so my squeak and I left the man and the girl with little more than a polite nod and a panicked look, hopefully well hidden behind my cotton face mask. I decided to take one last glance back as I left the airport. The girl was watching me with a smile. He looked as bewildered as me, as a sea of people from our plane was managing to do what I had not: navigate around them seamlessly.

The transfer driver had spelt my name quite wrong. How many Ls did Melodie Pelletier really need? Surely three was plenty? Apparently not. But I didn't care and I didn't correct the name scrawled on the sign. I was just happy to be away from the airport, away from England, and away from the strange encounter.

I was desperately trying to hold onto the driver's words while he chatted about practising his English. I think he said his name was Spiros. For the most part, the words were rushing past me with the people and the trees. He was a squat little man with one chubby hand on the steering wheel and the other waving around as he spoke. He looked as though he had somehow been condensing over time. I managed to absorb that his livelihood, like that of many others, had been hit by the recent pandemic and so now he was perfecting his English, and had taken on a second job as a driver. He was sweet and reminded me why I love Greek people so much: they are totally welcoming and totally free from the nonsense of the world. Perhaps those worry beads jangling from the mirror really did help. Maybe I should have got some.

We pulled up at my destination in a place called Astrakeri. As he took my bag from the boot of his well-kept Mercedes, the driver turned to me and gave me his card, sincerely reassuring me that if I needed anything to just call. He'd be happy to help. His kindness wasn't refreshing, not here in Corfu. It was the beautiful norm. Then he was gone, and I was alone.

Chapter 2

Weather-beaten. Yep, weather-beaten would definitely be the polite way to describe my home for the month. A very reasonably priced Airbnb for the size and location on the beach. Away from the world with a sea view. To me it was heaven. It didn't matter that the blue window frames hadn't been freshened up in quite some time and the classic whitewashed exterior needed some love.

Stepping into the manufactured chill gave me a deep sense of relief. I scanned the open-plan expanse of white walls and knick-knacks to find the key, a welcome pack, a set of instructions, and a forlorn cardboard box, all perched on the oddly modern breakfast bar. The lines of the room were very different to the unkempt exterior, clearly refurbished within the past few years. I picked up the key and ignored the papers. The owner had been very helpful and accepted extra payment to stock the fridge and leave a box of provisions before I arrived.

I slipped off my squeakers to feel the cool tiles beneath my puffy toes and wandered around upstairs to discover which of the three bedrooms was to be mine for the month. Each room was spacious but not ridiculously so. I couldn't pick between them so I dropped my bag in the last one I looked in. It had pale, sage-green linens with walls to match and a print of The Birth of Venus above the bed. She was proud yet coy about her nudity as she stood in her shell. For a moment I stood mindlessly looking at her, wondering if I'd chosen the right room. Turning my back on Venus and her friends, I placed my face mask away in a drawer. Time to be brave. One month. One month of further solitude. I'd made it out of my hole and into a fresh space. I had been frightened to leave my home, only removing myself for essentials, isolating for much longer than most. I needed this push.

Luckily for me, I could work from anywhere with Wi-Fi, giving me no attachments to worry about, so, when I decided to leave the house, I could go almost anywhere. I helped to craft other people's social media profiles. It paid well because I was good at it. I would create or encourage the creation of engaging content for various platforms, alongside knowing what posts to boost and when. It was flexible but painfully ironic work, given how antisocial I'd become.

After unpacking my things and exploring my new home, I sat outside on the step sipping some of the ouzo the owner had left me. Ouzo is a very important life essential in my opinion. A single dog walker strolled along the seafront; the beach was almost entirely lifeless as darkness began to reflect back at itself in the water.

In a week I'd be thirty-one and I had no one to call, no one who cared if I'd arrived safely, no one to worry about me. I let the ouzo rush through me quicker than I should have. The liquorice taste, strong and clear, brought forward past holidays

7

with my grandparents. I missed them terribly. I had lost them in the pandemic. My grandmama went first, after catching the horrific virus. It broke my grandpapa's heart; he just broke. He had a heart attack days later, unable to live without the love of his life. I hadn't seen either of them for a month at that point and it hurt my soul. It would always hurt my soul. They were the only parents I'd ever known. Their ghosts weighed heavily on my mind, as they so often did. The world was full of fresh sorrow with the loss of millions. I was but a drop in the ocean. People were starting to feel safe again. Most had for quite some time. I was the exception, not the rule. Not that feeling safe consoled me. How could it? It was hope for the future and regret for the past.

I inhaled the warm evening air, and it muddled itself with the ouzo fumes. During the heat of the day, it had been thirty-five degrees Celsius. After spending most of it in air-conditioned boxes, the thick sea air playing with the waves of my hair was like having a comforting hand on my neck. Reluctantly, after only a little more ouzo, I said goodnight to the comforting drone of the sea. I retreated to my new bedroom for a deep, exhaustion-induced sleep. I felt around for my phone in the dark: 3:33am. I looked at all of those threes in a daze. The air con had turned itself off and my sheets made me feel like the filling of a toasted sandwich. Placing my feet lightly on the tiles, still half asleep, and creeping pointlessly but habitually on tip-toe, I wandered along the landing and down the concrete staircase to find where to turn the air con back on. I stood still in my cotton nightshirt facing a little window. The moonlight was reflecting on the sea like shards of crystals sprawled on navy silk. It was too appealing.

I stepped out of the front door, creaking through the

shadows as I went. My toes felt their way, following the sandy dirt path towards the beach. The sand still held a comforting touch from the sun of the day, while the sea breeze soothed my skin. I kept walking, with the stars and the moon as my guide, down the beach and straight into the sea. My pale pink cotton nightshirt clung to me as the sea hit my thighs. I could see everything in a beautiful silver silhouette. I went under. For the longest second, I considered staying there. Suspended with the salt and the algae, the locks of my hazel hair stretching out, elegantly exploring like jellyfish tentacles.

Would anyone truly miss me? A few colleagues and one or two friends would cry but move on quickly, I was sure. My chest was slowly tightening. My mind lapsed into colours, green and turquoise, vivid cartoon memories of swimming in these very waters. Then there they were, in front of my eyes, part of the underwater world: my mama's laugh, the smell of mint from my papa all balled-up with the tension of my lungs. My tummy tightened yet my limbs were free. A sizeable fish brushed my leg and I instinctively shot out of the water. My lungs refilled with one sharp breath. The moment was gone. They were gone.

Refreshed to the point of freezing, I started walking back towards the beach, the see-through cotton of my nightshirt clinging to my body. I shivered in the night air, skin confused by the warmth and the night breeze. I stood outside the front door and slipped off my nightshirt, carefully placing it on the back of a chair on the porch. I didn't lock the door. I was more afraid of microbiology than anyone on the island. I quietly tip-toed back to bed, salty, damp and naked. It didn't matter – there was no one to worry about or to impress.

I woke up feeling gritty and disgusting. It was a good thing really; it meant I couldn't just lie there. I couldn't bear it. I got up, stripped the bed and jumped into the shower. Before I had sunk into the depths of my loneliness, I used to spring out of bed every day. Shower, make-up, hair, call Grandmama, make contact with clients, catch up with my personal socials…my own nine-to-five routine. Maybe not exactly like everyone else's Monday to Friday, as I'd worked from home for a long time, but pretty similar. Once Mama and Papa had gone, I had no one I wanted to call. I didn't want to get out of bed most days. I had got into the habit of reaching straight for my laptop, doing my work, making my calls, all in my bed, and only washing my hair and getting dressed if a video conference was on the cards. Other than that, I'd spent months in bed or on the sofa. Once, maybe twice, a week I'd force myself to run on the treadmill in my garage to stop my body turning completely to mush. I suppose even that was because I could hear my grandparents in the back of my mind. If I let myself go completely, and didn't look after myself, I'd be doing them a disservice. Even in death I didn't want to let them down.

I had intended to sunbathe and swim all day but a storm was rolling around on the sea. I sat on the porch as rain swept inwards. Patters spat up from the floor keeping my feet nicely wet. There was a flash of pink lightning, something I'd never seen before. Had I seen it at all? A magic firework across a gloomy grey? It made me feel too alone, mocked by the lightning forks, with their seemingly endless family members. I wanted to say, *Did you see that*? But who would answer? No one. I hadn't even spoken all morning. I often went for days without hearing my own voice.

The storm started to pull away from me, back out to sea. It

was all distant now, like my life. Everything I once had, now so out of reach. Not just unattainable, impossible. Don't get me wrong, I do love the drama of Corfu even the atmosphere holds entertainment. It doesn't matter if the sun's out or it's stormy. That's why it's so green and lush compared to other Greek islands. Even the pain of the storm gives hope for life. Then a purple flash, I remembered it all so vividly, like a dream that feels real and haunts you. But this was the opposite: real life that feels like a dream and stops you from sleeping.

After the storm, the weather picked up again, and I spent a few days swimming in the mostly deserted sea, drinking too much ouzo on ice and generally wandering around aimlessly. Then it was time. Time to go to the familiar old family haunt: Agios Stefanos.

11

Chapter 3

Even part way through the pandemic, tourists still went back to the beautiful, homely resort. Agios Stefanos had always had a chilled-out charisma that was hard to resist. I couldn't bring myself to stay there full-time though. Greeks always make you feel like a long-lost family member. The thing was, being welcomed like family when you have none of your own left was bound to be really hard. I had to psych myself up for it. Psych myself up for their full hearts and sad faces. Who really enjoys pity being projected onto them? I got into the taxi with only anxiety and ouzo in my belly. Not a good combination at eleven in the morning.

I wore flip-flops here. No squeaks, just flops. I slid my sunglasses over my eyes to shield them from the midday sun. Or that's what I told myself. The taxi dropped me off to stand with the cats. There have always been dozens of them at one particular spot. Tourists put food out, and a kind local takes donations to make sure the cats are cared for all year round. I just stood amongst them for a moment, amongst the curdled smell of sun-toasted cat food and the spit-roasted lamb from across the street. The cats didn't overly acknowledge me, being overfed by tourists in the summer months. I was staring at one little black kitten expertly cleaning its claws when my feet decided it was time to move. I walked towards Vicky's, the apartment blocks where we would so often stay. Maybe I'd just say hello there first and grab a drink at the pool bar. It seemed like the logical start point. Luckily Jenny, the receptionist, was there and she already knew my situation. No explanation necessary. Thank you, Facebook. She jumped up from behind her desk and came out from her glass bubble to greet me. Her pretty little face pulled into a tight frown as she held my hands and then embraced me with impressive might.

'I'm so sorry, Melodie.'

We'd never hugged in all the years we'd known each other. She was much shorter than me, almost a foot shorter in fact. She was perhaps four foot nine, with pale blue eyes and dirty-blonde hair. English by birth but Greek at heart. The resort wouldn't be the same without her. If you needed to know anything, you'd go straight to Jenny, no question. We'd only ever smiled and laughed together in the past. I could feel my eyes burning under my glasses.

'Come and have a drink. What would you like?' She led me like I was a child round the side of the reception to the bar.

'*Yassou*, Stavros.' I managed to lift my cheeks into a kind of smile.

'*Yassou*. How are you? I'm sorry for your grandparents.' Stavros held my hands across the solid wooden bar with no thought, only care. It was always going to be a long and painful day. He was Jenny's husband, a stocky man who stood eye level with me but was twice as broad. His soft brown eyes were warm and comforting. Tentatively, I let go of his hands and

13

pushed my hair behind my ears as some kind of emotional distraction. I went for an orange juice; my stomach was still churning from the days of ouzo, and it wasn't best pleased.

Almost forty minutes went by filled with moaning about the pandemic, chatting about the economy, the "new world" which mostly seemed pretty old, and generally putting it all to rights. I had managed to remove my sunglasses, and I appreciated the smell of gyros meat and cooking chips. Jenny had to go back to her receptionist duties, and I stayed for a salad. When it came, I had to smile. Placed down on the glass tabletop with a clang, it was huge: peppers, feta, olives, onions, cucumber – everything. Mama and I would always say we could split one at lunch, but we never did. We'd have both wanted all the feta and olives to ourselves. I was almost full at the halfway point, but I had to keep going; I'd got to be a little scrawny during the pandemic and had to buy new summer clothes, all size eight to ten. That's a little thin when you're five foot eight, or at least it was in my opinion. Not enough to make me shapeless, just thinner than I'd once been by a good ten pounds.

After the delicious delights of my salad, me and my food-baby belly made our way precariously to the beach. I wondered how my grandparents had made it down there in their early eighties. It was steep and narrow, a concrete slide with grit and sand that occasionally liked to act as little roller skates for your flip-flops. In quite recent times part of the walk down to the beach had been decked, but to be honest I sometimes found that portion even more dicey. My eyes were firmly on my feet until I made it to the bottom, the whole time trying not to gain speed for fear of never stopping. I knew that when I was eventually able to look up, it'd be there: the glistening Mediterranean Sea, and the sound of lapping water across the soft yet coarse golden sand. It must have been some time around two o'clock because the sand was scorching. Luckily, my body had already started to adjust over the past few days, including my skin, which was turning a nice golden brown. I started walking across the almost flaming sand down towards the relief of the sea. I hadn't brought any swimwear that day, just lotion, sunglasses, a shawl and a smattering of random make-up items, all in my petite beach bag. I put my feet in the water and watched the tourists. They were mostly middle-aged couples reading books or taking a refreshing dip in the turquoise water. There were a couple of young families interspersed with children giggling and running through the puddles left by the sea. A slice of Greek heaven. I decided to walk along, feet in the water, holding my flip-flops in one hand and the bottom of my dress in the other. Occasionally the breeze would brush locks of my shoulder-length hair across my face. It looked like an idyllic moment. The fact was, this image was completely scuppered each time I had to remove my hair from my face. It was not an elegant sight, trying to use either my flip-flop hand, which felt like someone was trying to kick me in the face, or trying to use my dress hand without showing the world my knickers. I felt my cheeks burn, and told myself it was the sun. I made a sharp dash left, off the beach, past a restaurant called Waves and up onto the road. At least then I could put my shoes back on and feel less on show.

Ambling upwards along the road didn't cause too much interruption from cars. It left space for my mind to wander too. During the previous days my brain had mostly gone between three things: work, my grandparents and the pair from the airport. His sharp jaw-line and muscular build. Her inquisitive but knowing looks, and their matching deep-green eyes. They made me feel rather bland. My hair and eyes were both naturally pale hazel-brown; nothing as striking as a deep-emerald shade. That's not to say I hadn't had my fair share of compliments over the years. My doll eyes were usually the subject of compliments. I liked to emphasise their bush baby look with layers of mascara even on the lower lashes.

Then, he appeared – as though I'd called upon him and he had manifested. I stopped in the dust at the side of the road among insects and discarded cigarette butts. He was much more impressive than I had remembered. Exceptionally tall with a rugged refinement, hair softly set in place but a face ready for action, and fierce, striking bone structure. Suddenly his working frown erupted into a laugh with an exchange from a passer-by. In essence though, he was just there, just unloading something from a van at one of my favourite restaurants, Fantasea. With his skin glistening, presumably from the sweat of his labours, to me he looked perfectly, almost intentionally, oiled. I'd never seen anyone quite like him, and I was in awe. The restaurant name felt painfully and ridiculously apt in that moment.

His black-brown hair was being ruffled by the breeze and his tan was deeper than before. My heart was pounding in my throat as I spun around on my heels. I didn't want to be noticed so I just stood looking over towards the sea. I'd made the walk high enough up the road that the view looking down on the bay was incredible. So, fortunately for me, staring at it was completely credible. I was clutching my bag tightly, so tightly that it dug in and hurt a little. My mind was racing. What do I do? Do I say something? Do I carry on walking? Likely he wouldn't recognise me anyway. I'd been wearing a mask when he saw me last and although I like my doe eyes, I doubt them to be as memorable as his.

I started to grope aggressively in my bag for my compact. Found! Then a quick sneaky glance to check my mascara hadn't migrated away from where I put it, and that my pale coral lipstick had made it through lunch. Check! Then to carefully use said mirror to look behind me. There was nothing. I spun around to see the little van making its way down the hill. All I could think was: how is any of this possible? That he was here in the first place – there were dozens of beautiful beach resorts in Corfu. It wasn't the biggest Greek island, but it was nowhere near the smallest. Did I just imagine him? Perhaps the months and months of being alone, combined with the heat, had made me hallucinate. Maybe I'd been too hopelessly focused on him and now my brain was adding him into random places when it was bored.

Then I was walking, fast. Likely too fast. My feet were rushing down the slope, so much so that I was running the risk of losing one of my tatty little flip-flops. The van was there, stopped outside one of the little supermarkets helping Demetris with some oranges. What was I doing? Why was I stalking him? I couldn't sensibly answer that, not even now. At least he hadn't been some strange manifestation; he was real after all. Thankfully, he didn't have the girl with him to give me another soul inspection. No, I was wrong again. That's when I saw her reflection in the wing mirror of his van. Sitting in the passenger seat singing along to whatever was playing. I spun around again to face the other way. I frantically fanned my face as the sweat clung to my skin. Had I travelled through time to be a fourteen-year-old girl again? Staying away from people for such an expanse of time meant, I had forgotten how to behave. I could hear footsteps rushing towards me, slapping

17

against the pavement. Was it her? Had she seen me? What should I do?

Chapter 4

'There you are!' A familiar voice and arms suddenly around me from behind... Maria. It was Maria, Jenny and Stavros's daughter. Five years my junior and five inches shorter than me, so significantly taller than her mother. Her arms were holding me tightly from behind, pinning me to the spot, with her cool cheek pressed into my back. 'I've been looking for you! Mum said you were here!' She squealed and squeezed even tighter.

'Hi, Maria.' I sounded hoarse from the lack of air in my lungs.

She swung me round to face her, or to look down at her. Instead, I was looking over her head. The van was off once more and I was none the wiser. Perhaps that was a good thing.

'I'm so sorry about Pip and Pete,' she continued. 'We'll raise a glass or six to them tonight, yes?'

'Sounds good to me,' I said, brought back to her by the sound of my grandparents' names.

In our younger years we had spent a good few nights out drinking together and persuading local boys and tourists to buy us cocktails, or bottles of ouzo from the little supermarkets to drink on the beach. Mostly it's an older demographic for a resort, but we made it our own. We were chalk and cheese to look at in many ways. She had inherited Jenny's blonde hair, but brighter, and slight hips and busty frame. I was tall, lean, with an almost, but not quite, hourglass shape, and pretty much as slim as back when we'd met, without my mama to feed me up. When she was seventeen, I was twenty-two and we thought we ruled Agios Stefanos that summer. It's her fault I like ouzo so much. We played cards on the beach and drank until late most nights.

'How've you been, girl? You look thin. Why didn't you message me to say you were coming? Why aren't you staying at Vicky's?' She was walking me along arm in arm back down the slope, back the way I had come. Through the smell of tomatoey Greek stews and cooking meat from the restaurants and fresh fruits and vegetables in the supermarkets. All quietly getting ready for the evening rush.

'I couldn't face it. I'm not staying too far away. An Airbnb in Astrakeri right on the beach. It has three bedrooms. You should visit me for a change!' I said, and nudged her lightly in the ribs with the arm she was still clinging to.

'I'm offended!'

'No, you're not.'

'I could be.' She paused long enough for me to see it again, the van. No sign of people though. 'I'll take you up on that. How long are you here?' She was still talking, but my eyes were fixed on the van and my breath had stopped. Where had they gone? Were they nearby?

'Melo! Are you listening?' Maria said, fingers pulsing on my arm.

'Sorry, yes. A month.' My voice came out in a very stunted whisper, and my hands were sweating again. Why was I having such a strong reaction to these people? I was being outrageously ridiculous. Just keep walking, forget about them, I told myself. I did it. I walked past and didn't even look back. I suppressed my intrigue like a grown-up. I still don't know how. As we marched down the street, I realised this was truly the longest anyone had touched me in so long. I couldn't remember how long it'd been. It felt equally familiar and alien.

'It'll just be us tonight, Harry is working.' Maria was engaged to the lovely Harry. He had visited Agios Stefanos with his parents and fell for Maria within the week. She was twenty-three when they met. He was only twenty-one and straight from finishing a degree in business. He dropped all of his job opportunities to take a gap year and get bar work on the island. That was three years ago and he was still in Corfu, much to the horror and delight of his parents. He might not earn the money of London, but they seemed damn happy to me.

'I'll have to do with just you then, I guess.'

'Sorry about that!' She smiled out of the corner of her mouth and pushed her soft blonde hair over her shoulder. 'I've taken so long to find you I'll have to go back to work now.'

'Well, we're almost there. Where do you want to meet? Do you want to have some dinner?' I grinned, knowing this was a loaded question. She let out a small snort.

'Let's say Vicky's around seven.' We air-kissed, and she slipped into the jeweller's where she worked part-time. It's funny we would only see each other perhaps once a year or so, yet we had known each other for almost ten years. Some people feel like a puzzle piece of the sky, or the grass. They aren't really the focus of the puzzle, but you'd soon notice if

21

they weren't there.

The first time we met was at Vicky's one quiet evening. I'd sent my grandparents off for a romantic meal as an anniversary gift. It was our first trip to Agios Stefanos, so I just stayed at Vicky's to enjoy the view before getting an early night. That was the plan until a little blonde madam stormed up to the bar buzzing away. I couldn't work out if she was angry, telling a story or just liked waving her arms a lot. I had no clue, but I remember just watching her with fascination. Unfortunately, or what turned out to be fortunately, she noticed my obvious stare.

'Can I help you?' Her tone was pleasant; her eyes were not.

I choked on my drink as she took a step towards me. It didn't matter that she was tiny and pretty – her personality could fill a concert hall. She wore a tight red dress, with matching lipstick, and a wide, pointless black belt around her straight waist. Her hand was clutching the bar, but she was steady.

'No, sorry. I – I was just wishing I spoke Greek, I guess. I didn't mean to intrude.'

Her face changed quickly, and the muscles in her jaw relaxed as she gave a little tut of the tongue. It was like being back at the airport, walking through the metal detector, as, with a flash of false lashes, she scanned me for issues.

'Maria,' she said, with a nod.

'Melodie.'

'Ha! I like that name. Melodie. Okay, Melodie, I was telling my father here that I wanted to go to a party tonight, and he told me I should be studying. That's what was going on. Which, by the way, means I'm going to a party. Wanna come with? You look pretty lonely.'

'Pretty or lonely?' I smiled at her, and she shrugged with a grin.

'Just lonely,' she said, and that was that really. I couldn't dare to say no to her, if her own father couldn't manage to – so, I went along.

We smoked cigarettes, drank too much, laughed at nothing, and danced more than I ever had before. It wasn't until later that evening that I got the nickname "Melo". It was my first time having jelly shots and I showed quite a taste for them. For a time there, I was "Melo-Jello", which luckily didn't have staying power.

Walking away from the jeweller's, I felt lucky I'd met her. It was nice to have a link with someone here. I decided to go to a few bars and have the awkward "they died" talk with some of the owners and workers. Big smiles crumpled into frowns in seconds. The Greeks are so family-oriented, so caring. I had no idea how they managed to remember so many people, stories, lives.

When it was done, I started wandering the main road like a nomad again, slower than ever, flip-flops scraping along the tatty tarmac and hands back to clinging to my bag, reminiscing about laughter and good times we'd had. A snowball was building in my gut with every thought, tight and cold.

I was dreaming of the time when we had just got to within two metres of the restaurant Little Prince and a bird pooed all over Papa's head. Mama and I cackled and winced, tears of laughter cooling our cheeks as we doubled over. It took another day for him to see the funny side though. His face was still, almost steamrollered at the whole thing, which just made us laugh more. Looking into Zorbas, I could see my grandparents again, table-tapping and whooping as the staff set fire to pretty much anything and everything for our entertainment. Peering across the tables as I passed, I had to bite my cheek at the sight of the phallic-looking cacti on some of the tables, which I had always giggled at every time we were there.

Walking past Olympia and their giant pots, all the waiters waved to me. Then I was back in my mind, passing more tavernas and shops, letting people, cats and cars roam past me. I had started to make my way back up to the small church. I'd never actually been inside it before; I'd only admired it from afar. The building was a traditional white and pale blue, with an archway to walk through to get to the door. As I passed beneath it, I took my cream spotted shawl from my bag and placed it carefully around my shoulders.

The church was very small and busier than I'd expected – not with people, but with pictures, shrines and lots of gold. I didn't really know what I had expected. The outside was so calm and quiet, the interior busy and vibrant. The only sounds were those of a grasshopper and the distant sea. I wanted to sit and clear my mind, but my mind was as busy as the walls. Every time I tried, I started to think about the beautiful tall man and Gaia, the Greek mother of all life; or was she just a twelve-year-old girl? Who knew? I didn't. I closed my eyes and inhaled deeply the smell of wooden chairs, that had all been perfectly set out in rows and melting candle wax typical of churches the world over. Their candles providing a warm glow of reassurance and comfort to all who enter.

I sat for some time on a hard wooden chair. At the apex of the front wall was a painting of an eye. Watching over the church. Watching over me from inside its white triangle. It's dark, aged paint made it almost menacing, the weighted eyelid pressing downwards, perhaps puffy from tears.

I spent quite some time looking at the eye before I stood up to leave. Putting some change in a big wooden box, I took a candle for myself. I could feel my abdomen tighten, and I held my breath. My hand shook a little as I tried to light the candle. Loss is the biggest realisation that no one truly has control over anything. The pandemic had done that too, of course. The eye studied me as I took my last look across the interior.

I slowly exited the church into the heat of the evening and the buzz of electricity and insects. Time was getting on, and I had to walk all the way back down the slope, following the road round to Vicky's bar. I removed my shawl and took a leisurely pace, bag pressed to my side, arms folded across my chest. I had hoped to cleanse my mind fully of thought, but it hadn't worked.

I paused in the lay-by opposite Fantasea restaurant again to absorb the irresistible view of the bay below. The sun was beginning to hang low in the sky to the side, but it still sat within its bright blue bed, with a skimpy orange cloud as a blanket. I took a step to walk away but got my foot caught in some old fishing line. I hopped forward trying to free my foot, I stuttered along, then my bag dropped forwards taking me with it. I skidded along the dirt on my right knee then my palms.

Like a child, my eyes began to tingle and itch. My breath caught in my chest, somewhere between a juddered snuffle and a sniff. I pulled at the wire, which had tucked itself into the front of my flip-flop, and I tried to throw it with all my force, only for it to whip and float in a delicate swirl. It came to rest no more than a foot away from me. I didn't know whether to laugh or cry. My palms stung and my knee throbbed. What a fool. What a bloody fool! I rolled onto my bottom and clutched my knee, pressing hard into the tender flesh to suppress the sensation.

'Are you okay?' The voice came from above.

Great. It wasn't enough to fall over, or to be fighting back tears, but someone had to witness the spectacle. Fantastic.

'I'm fine, thank you,' I called back, without looking up. It was just my luck. I could hear their feet dancing towards me with a swift beat. Just what I didn't want. 'Seriously, I –' I turned and looked up. It was him. Him from the airport. Him from the van. He was by my side, kneeling next to me. His eyes became as wide as mine – they looked almost golden as the evening sun giggled its way across his skin.

'It's you! Oh well, at least I didn't knock you over this time.' His voice had a note of Greek to it and his full lips softly curled up. Large warm hands were on my arms again, helping me up this time, gently lifting me to my feet, as though I were as hollow as a bird's bone.

'No Gaia?' I said, looking past him towards Fantasea, waiting to see if she was staring down from their restaurant area.

His smile got broader at the mention of her name.

'No, no. She is with her friends.'

'Oh.' I didn't know what I'd expected. Perhaps that she was practising how to part the sea somewhere. Or something equally ridiculous.

'How's your knee? Are you okay?'

'I'm fine. Honestly.' I was acutely aware he was still holding my arm. I prayed he would let go before he noticed the breakneck speed of my pulse. I pulled away.

'Thank you though.' I turned away from him and began to walk. My face was twisted, my eyes wide and my fingers couldn't help but cover my mouth.

'Wait, do you need a lift? Your knee is bleeding. I have a first-aid kit in my van.'

I stopped to look down at my knee. So it was – bleeding. What did I have to lose? I had nothing. Nothing worth having. My eyes squinted then fixed back on him, almost a silhouette in the sun. My words came out faint, distant, isolated somewhere far away from who I once was.

'That'd be lovely, thank you.'

Chapter 5

His van smelt of coffee and damp air conditioning. Both were unsurprising. The doors were littered with single-use coffee cups, crushed ready for the bin. He got in next to me and shut the door, his first-aid kit on his lap.

'I didn't catch your name at the airport. I'm Anton, or Ant for short if you prefer.'

It couldn't be a more ironic name, given his size. His broad shoulders more than filled his seat and he made his first-aid box look like a child's toy. I gave a snort of disbelief, and he rolled his eyes just as quickly.

'I know, I know. Ironic. I've heard it all before. Stupid name if you ask me.'

The last part he muttered under his breath while continuing his rummaging. His black sleeveless top and shorts looked fresh and clean, which was impressive in the heat and dust. Other than his size and his eyes, he looked pretty Greek. He was rugged, with dark hair and thick brows, and a little on the hairy side. His strong jaw was hidden beneath his almost-beard. Then his large hands were fiddling, trying desperately to open a little sachet containing an antibacterial wipe.

'Melodie,' I said. 'And I don't mind the name Anton. It suits you.' While suppressing a giggle, I held out my hand automatically.

He took it tentatively.

'It seems a long time since I've shaken someone's hand.'

Corfu hadn't been badly hit by the pandemic but social distancing, and other tight rules, had been in place from the start.

'I didn't even think! It was automatic. Sorry,' I said and pulled my shoulders up into a little shrug.

He managed to prise open the little packet and extract the wipe. He carefully passed it to me with a smile.

'That's okay. I trust you.' There was more weight to his voice than I'd have expected for a comment so flippant. Unless it was just my imagination and wishful thinking. 'Plus, I've knocked into you, helped you up twice, and now you're sat in my van. It's a bit late to care.'

After I had wiped my knee, he passed me a rather large plaster, much larger than required. I carefully placed it on my right knee with a little pat. Even though it dominated my knee, with very little sympathy for my vanity, I didn't want to offend his kindness.

'So?' His deep-green eyes were piercing through me again, down to my soul.

'So?' I mimicked vacantly. My heart was still pounding and the air conditioning hadn't prevented my hands from sweating. The sweat was making my palms sting as the salt tormented my poor little grazes. I absentmindedly wiped them across the material on my thighs. Thankfully it didn't mark the soft navy chiffon of my dress, even with the dirt from the ground mixed with my sweat. I was looking down, wishing I'd worn something a little more impressive. It was a nice dress, though, but quite plain – strappy, not quite a low neckline, short at the front and floating down at the back. That's when I realised that we were sitting in silence while I over-analysed myself. He was just watching me with a half-smile on his face.

'Are you not going to tell me where you need to be?'

My face felt like its temperature had gone up another ten degrees or so.

'Oh! Sorry, yes, Vicky's.' What an idiot. At least he didn't dwell on it. He just began to turn his van around. I was grateful not to have his eyes on me.

'Vicky's is nice.' he said. 'Have you stayed there before?'

'Many times, but not today,' I said, with a smile over my round lips. I lightly touched them and wondered how my lipstick was looking.

'Really? Where are you staying, then?'

'Astrakeri.'

'Nice area. How long are you staying for?'

Was it just polite conversation or was he actually interested? I hoped he was interested. I was pulling gently at the hem of my dress so as not to stare at him. His hair was neatly cut but a little longer on top. I just wanted to touch it.

'A month, or thereabouts.'

'All on your own?' He gave me a little sideways glance. He definitely seemed interested in what my answer would be.

'Yes, but I'm meeting a friend at Vicky's.'

We were almost there already. This little meeting had been both embarrassing and short. I'd hoped that if we had interacted again, I'd at least come across as mildly elegant, or at the very least, not a buffoon. Too late for that – I'd already been seen for who I've always been: clumsy.

He drove down the dirt road to the apartment blocks and stopped next to the surrounding wall. He twisted to face me while he drummed his fingers on the wheel absent-mindedly. Then I noticed. How had I not noticed before? I obviously hadn't wanted to notice. A wedding ring. In Greece they wear their wedding ring on the right; I had known that, but up to that point I had conveniently forgotten. Of course he was married. Gaia was clearly his daughter. Based on looks alone, there was never a doubt of that. So why hadn't I thought him to be married? Probably because I didn't want him to be.

'Thank you for the lift...' I started to open the door. '...And the plaster. It was very kind of you.'

I got out, but just as I went to slam the door shut, he leant across my seat.

'Wait! Will you be in Agios Stefanos again? Will I see you?'

'I'm not sure your wife would approve.' I turned on my flip-flops and attempted my sexiest storm-off walk. I'm still not sure if that's actually a thing, but it's what I was trying to achieve. I heard the van steadily pull away and my heart promptly sank. Oh well, another little dream crushed. It had been nice while it lasted. I might never understand his daughter's eyes, but I'd understood his and adultery wasn't a life complication I needed.

It was nice to laugh. Maria didn't sit around pitying me. That was not her way. We sat at a table in the bar area after being fed to the brim with delicious souvlaki, feta, tzatziki, more salad, chips and rice! Perhaps not quite the brim, as we still had room for cocktails. Her laugh made me laugh even more, with an out-of-breath snort.

'Come on, let's go.' she grabbed my bag from the floor and

started to march off.

'Wait for me, then!' I scrambled to my feet and was off after her.

'Where are we going, then?'

'Condor? I hear Lady Gaga is there tonight.'

'Oh well, we don't have much choice then, do we?'

Our march advanced at quite a pace, and we continued to laugh as we went over the bridge and past all the cats.

'I think Rihanna should be there tonight too, you know,' Maria stated very matter of fact, with a pause before laughing again.

When we arrived at the bar, it was buzzing. It wasn't as busy as I'd seen it in the past but everyone was smiling, laughing and many were dancing. Every other person was singing along, or swaying, or pointing their finger to the beat. The bass vibrated my chest. It was early still, maybe around half nine, something like that and we were already a little drunk. Maria started flinging her hair from side to side, shoulders bouncing to the music. I went to the bar.

'Two Sexy Greeks, please,' I said, with a tiny slur.

I got a wink and a smile before he went off to make the cocktails. The tribute act was halfway through "Bad Romance" when I got our drinks. Maria grabbed her drink in one hand and me in the other. We were shouting the words and dancing; limbs were flying everywhere, as were our drinks. When the singer went on her break, Mud's "Tiger Feet" came on. Maria started jumping up and down, laughing and kicking her feet all over the place! She was unstoppable. Suddenly she was up on top of a table and pulling me up with her. I was laughing so hard my sides ached. She was swinging her feet about so frantically to the music, one of her flip-flops flew off her foot and hit a man square in the back of his bald little head! He spun around, literally not knowing what had hit him! She jumped off the table, grabbed his little shiny head and kissed it, apologising, almost thrusting the poor man into her bosom – much to the irritation of his wife. I could feel tears of laughter streaming down my face. I climbed down, apologising to the people who had been sitting at the table, gulped down my drink and pulled Maria away.

'Athens Bar?' I shouted over the music and laughter.

She grinned with a nod. She was still hurling apologies over her shoulder as we left while clutching her partner in crime, her flip-flop.

Athens Bar had a live band on, too; it was more loud music and dancing. All ages in together. That's something I had always loved about Greece. It's like there is no age gap between people. It's just people and family. Respect for all. I will always love that. We danced until we could feel our feet aching in spite of the alcohol filter. Sometime in the early hours we found ourselves lying on the beach talking, just like we had all those years ago.

'Thank you...' I paused. 'It's nice to be drunk with someone else. It's been weird,' I slurred.

'So weird!' She sat up, throwing her arms to the sky. 'Wait, what's been weird?' she burst into fits of giggles.

'You, silly arse, the pandemic nonsense and life and stuff.' I looked up into the sky, trying to focus on the stars above, wishing they would ground me and stop bloody spinning.

'It's okay.' She looked over at me. 'You're here now. Nothing better than Greek food, booze and people to soothe a soul.' She gently tapped me on the forehead and laughed again.

I closed my eyes, because the stars had started to taunt me,

33

and I didn't appreciate it one bit.

'I can see how sad you are, you know, Melo. It's more than your grandparents, isn't it?' She spoke softly through her own little boozy slur.

'Maybe. You're the first person I've spent time with in a long while. The pandemic just made it easier for me to slip away, you know? Easier to shut people out. I'm just sick of being lonely and afraid of people. That's why I pushed myself to come back here, you know? Make or break or something? You know?' My eyes were shut but I was frowning as I spoke. It was more than I meant to say, but that's alcohol.

'I know. I hear you, girl,' she said. 'You need a boyfriend.'

She laughed and lay back down next to me. She'd oversimplified my issues somewhat, but in essence she wasn't wrong. After that, it was a blur. I don't remember if we kept on talking or if I just fell asleep in the sand.

'Hello, you two.'

'I know that voice,' I croaked, without opening my eyes. The sun was warming my lids as I accepted the fact we had fallen asleep on the beach and stayed there. 'Hi, Harry. Do you happen to have any water?' I sat up slowly and looked across to see Maria still asleep with an arm over her eyes.

'Fun night?'

'Yeah, from what I remember.' I was looking at him with one eye closed. 'How are you, anyway?'

'Good, thanks. I was sorry to hear about your grandparents. They were good people.' He was still standing over us but dropped his smirk to a more serious nod.

'Help me up. I need to go back to my house.'

He pulled me up and nearly fell backwards himself. We stumbled to the music of Maria laughing at us. When we came to a stop, we were eye to eye, almost the same height. My body was swaying, wanting to fall back down into the warm embrace of the sand. Then my blood pressed into my brain with a harsh throb, like bubbles swelling and popping at my temples.

'Arrrggh,' was all I could manage. Maria and Harry both laughed. 'Thanks, you arseholes. I don't know why you're laughing. You haven't stood up yet!' I started forcefully pointing at Maria, who stopped laughing and continued hiding behind her arm.

Harry offered me a lift and I happily accepted. We left Maria on the beach to find her own way home. As soon as I got into Harry's little Corsa, I felt worse. I hadn't thought it would be possible. We both had our windows gaping open, and his coiled brown hair bouncing and dancing in the breeze.

'Here.' He grabbed a bottle of water from the back seat and threw it onto my lap.

'Yes! Thank you so much!'

'So how's life in England been?'

'Ermm, to be honest' —I gulped water frantically— 'I feel like I wouldn't know. I wasn't one of the people going to the pubs when they opened.' I laughed, but the reality was I'd stayed months longer than most other than for essentials. I hadn't wanted to be with people for a very long time. 'How've you been? Maria seems very happy.' I sipped the water then hunched forwards to watch huge birds of prey through the windscreen, circling high above.

'We're good. It's been a while since I've seen her that hung over, though!' The rest of the journey followed on in polite conversation, which still made my head hurt. As soon as I got back to the house, I washed and went to bed.

When I awoke it was abruptly, not knowing where I was. I looked around with that dreadful confused sensation. I'd been dreaming of my grandparents and the girl, Gaia. I sat for a moment clutching my knees. I dreamt they had led me to her and passed me her hand. I didn't understand it, but I let myself cry.

Two days until my birthday. I was sitting on the beach listening to the waves and staring at the sand, rubbing small quantities between my fingers, enjoying the crunching before releasing it back to the beach. Thirty-one wasn't old, but I felt so left behind. I didn't want to let myself be a cliché, but I did want someone to share my time with. Most of my work colleagues and friends from school were married or had children, or both. Not all, but most.

Chapter 6

Waking up alone on my birthday without a card or a gift was odd. If I were at home and not in Corfu I'd likely have had quite a few cards at the very least. They would be waiting for me on the mat at home. As it was, all I had were Facebook messages and Instagram stories containing happy photos from long before the pandemic.

I knew how I was going to spend the day; I'd planned it months before. Like most days, I'd start on the beach, but that night I'd take myself to Yiannis Family Restaurant in Agios Stefanos. It'd be busy enough that I'd be able to happily sit alone without too much fuss and I could people-watch too. It was a place we liked to go because always, without fail, we would get a free slice of Greek orange cake. Everyone did. That was to secretly be my birthday cake, and I was very much looking forward to it. The taxi was booked – I just had eleven hours to fill before it arrived. I planned on getting dressed up. My heels were coming out – not the squeaky pair, the purple-and-pink strappy ones. I'd laid out a wraparound dress with spaghetti straps. It was Cadbury's purple, low-cut, and emphasised my waist and hips. I was excited to wear it at last. It was nice to be wearing something other than my usual fluffy loungewear.

When I arrived back in Agios Stefanos, people were already out wandering, deciding where to eat. I stepped out of the taxi and was engulfed by the hubbub pouring out from every bar and restaurant. Every step held something different, as each taverna had its own mouth-watering atmosphere, from loud traditional music with clapping and dancing, to the quiet and understated with ornamental pots with the warm smell of chicken in a cream and mushroom sauce. Then on to pork chops the size of a forearm.

I was given a table at the side of the restaurant, outside of course. It was exactly as I had expected. I people-watched, had a fragrant moussaka with aubergines topping the scent of lamb and oregano. Then, I waited for my cake. Another "Happy Birthday" message on Facebook popped up on my phone. When I looked up, he was standing across from me. Anton. He was hovering over my table. I looked up, my mouth a little open. I started looking about only to find people glancing at me – the people who I was there to watch – this broad, dark figure had drawn their attention to me.

'May I sit down?'

'I don't know. What would your wife say?' My tone was coarse, my lips pulled tight and I narrowed my eyes at him for emphasis.

'Not much, I'm sure.' He sat down opposite me as he spoke. He was all in black again but this time a fitted short-sleeve shirt. 'I hope you don't mind. I was just dropping off Gaia at her friend's when I saw you here.' I didn't reply. What was the point? He was married. The waitress placed my cake in front of me and smiled. She said something in Greek to Ant. He returned her smile, shook his head and said what I think was 'No, thank you' in Greek.

'What do you want?' The adrenaline pulsing through my body was much higher than it should have been. He was just so beautiful it hurt. I looked down at my cake, inhaled the rich, sticky, orange scent, picked up my fork and took a bite. I wasn't going to let him ruin the enjoyment of my birthday treat.

'I'm a widower,' he said.

At that, I sharply inhaled a crumb. Short, raspy coughs came through my teeth as I desperately tried not to spit cake all over him. I pressed my hands to my mouth as my chest jolted to remove the little crumb from its little escapade. Unfortunately for me, Anton jumped up, pushing his chair to the floor and started tapping me on the back. I choked a little harder at this but mostly due to embarrassment.

'I'm fine,' I said through gritted teeth and cake before managing to swallow. 'Please God, sit down!' He did as he was told, picking up his chair and giving dainty looks to our new onlookers. The waitress was also looking to check I was okay, so I snatched the opportunity to ask for another bottle of wine and another glass. I grabbed my handbag, shamelessly slipped out my compact and checked my face. This would not be the time to have dribble on my chin or mascara smudges from watery eyes. Matte, pink lipstick, mascara and eyeshadow were all still in place. I tried to pull back what damage I had done by offering my sympathy and finding out what had happened.

'A heart attack. She was outwardly healthy. Apparently, she had a genetic weakness and she just died. Gaia was only three.

39

She was the only one there when it happened.' I swallowed hard then pressed my teeth into my cheeks. He hadn't looked me in the eye while saying his words. He was looking at his wedding ring, circling it with his thumb. Luckily the extra wine arrived and the waitress poured Ant a glass.

'I'm so, so sorry.'

'I know it's been ten years,' —I mentally noted that Gaia must be thirteen, then; my guess about her age hadn't been too wrong— 'but I wear the ring for Gaia to show her that her mother doesn't go forgotten.'

'That makes sense. She is lucky to have you.'

'I don't know about that.' He took a deep gulp of wine.

I wasn't the only one with too much weighing on their heart and their mind.

'So...' I looked at him over my wine.

'So...' he repeated. 'I'm sorry to intrude on your cake. I just didn't want you to think I'm some sort of cheater, flirting with you,' he said, but the word "flirting" lingered in the air between us.

'You're actually intruding on my birthday cake. And that's exactly what I thought.' I pointed my fork in his direction as I spoke. 'Birthday cake?' He raised a thick eyebrow at me in disbelief.

'Yes. Is that a problem?'

'No, just a surprise. No one to celebrate with?'

I didn't want to completely step on his cheeky smile, so I went with a simple "No," and finished my cake.

'Do you want me to leave? It's obviously a choice to be alone.'

'I wouldn't say that...No, you're fine.' The turmoil in my stomach from seeing him again was settling. I wondered how he felt about me. He had asked to see me again previously, although, for all I knew it was for some crazed or malicious reason. That would be based solely on the way his daughter stared at me in the airport. The way her eyes scanned me, like she was going to make a replica of me as a toy.

'If you're sure?' He seemed timid, which I found very amusing with his imposing stature. He wasn't overly musclebound. It looked more natural than that, as though he didn't have to try or work too hard to be so finely sculpted.

'I'm sure.' We sat silently for a moment both totally unsure of ourselves.

'Tell me where you're from.' Someone had to start, and it might as well be me.

'Well, my father is English and my mother Greek. I was born in Essex, but we moved out here when I was a toddler and we've lived between the two on and off.'

'That makes sense. That's why you don't have a strong accent and go to England on holiday when you already live in paradise.'

'Exactly. We try to see my parents at least twice a year. They come here, we go there.'

'What made them name you Anton, do you think?'

He looked down at the table and started playing with a napkin holder, shuffling it back and forth with a smile. 'Good question! My mother wanted to call me Antis, but she didn't win. There was a compromise involved, I believe.'

'Which do you prefer? Are you glad she didn't win?'

'Honestly? Neither would be my choice, but I don't really care It's just a bit ironic. I got my dad's height and I guess they didn't think about the nickname "Ant" for someone who might be tall.' He gave a little smirk with a distant look of someone considering something affectionately, then his eyes snapped back to me. 'So, what about you? Where are you from?'

'Oh, nowhere interesting. I've lived in a small village outside of Cambridge my whole life.' He topped up my glass again. We were both using sipping our wine as a glass wall to hide behind. Alas, as with any glass wall, there was no real hiding, it was obvious.

'So, what brings you to Corfu for your birthday?'

'I'm actually a regular to Agios Stefanos. I used to come here all the time with my grandparents. They passed away during the pandemic, so I wanted to come and...I don't know really, escape home. Escape from myself. Which of course is completely impossible!' The wine was clearly doing its job at last; I was becoming more open with each passing millisecond.

'I'm sorry to hear that.'

'You lost your wife. I can't moan –'

'Don't be ridiculous. Everyone's life is different and should be embraced.' It dawned on me it'd take a lot more wine for him not to feel sensible than it would me. Not that I couldn't hold my drink – I could. But I was a skinny five-foot-eight woman and he was a bulky six-foot-four man. I had little chance of drinking him under the table anytime soon.

'I take it you were close to them?'

'They brought me up. I never knew my parents. My mother, their daughter, left me not long after I was born. She was only a child herself really, just sixteen. She left and never came back.' I started to twist the silver ring on my right hand with my thumb, a gift from Mama and Papa on my sixteenth birthday. A delicate little ring with a blue-green opal in the centre.

'That's dreadful. I can't imagine.' His brows drew tightly together, a look I'd seen on people's faces my entire life; it's not just a pity look, it's more than that. I think perhaps it's

42

shock. He did look a little shocked. It's there in the dark of people's eyes.

'Yep, unwanted then, unwanted now, always alone.'

'You're not unwanted and you're not alone!' He sat heavily back in his chair, shaking his head. Then a shy expression darted across his face, just for a moment, before his fingers touched his beautiful lips. I blushed and quickly called the waitress over to break the fluster and asked for the bill. We were linked in bashfulness if nothing else.

'You must let me pay, as a birthday gift.'

'Don't be silly. I don't even know you and you didn't even get any dinner!'

'Okay, well, where shall we go next? I have to at least buy you another drink.' I took a moment to study his face. He was almost pleading with me, eyes wide, posture forward and persuasive. Not that I needed persuading.

'Fine. But somewhere that isn't too loud.'

The bill was paid and we found ourselves walking towards Athens Bar. It was a lot quieter without live music, more atmospheric, as long as we stayed outside. He grabbed my hand as we stepped under the archway, entering the patio area, and walked me to the right, to a table outside. His touch totally threw me and I could feel a throb in my head as desire washed over me.

At a small, round table for two, he pulled out a white director's-style chair for me. I sat down carefully, tucking my dress under me and watched him as he moved around the table. I fluffed up my hair, hoped there was nothing in my teeth, and knew I wanted him. But I also knew I could never have him. I wasn't a holiday fling type. Particularly with someone who had a young daughter. Especially a young, slightly creepy one. On the other hand, I was happy to indulge in a flirtation; it was my birthday after all.

'Is Gaia out for the night then?'

'Yep. Since getting out of lockdown all she wants to do is see her friends. She's thirteen, so I think it's normal to enjoy her freedom…and pushing me. I can't blame her. Lockdown was very hard here. Even to go to the supermarket you would have to text a number about it. She's at another sleepover tonight. I find it hard to let go, I quite liked hanging out with her in lockdown.'

'That's normal though. I would wager having a six-foot-four dad holds the boys at bay at least?' I shot him a cheeky smile and leant back in my chair. He gave a rugged little chuckle that carried on the bass-line of the music.

'Not as much as I'd like.' He rubbed his stubbled chin. His smile was wide and endearing. 'Six foot four and a half actually…' We were interrupted momentarily to give our drinks order. I looked away as I ordered a Sexy Greek. I wanted to giggle but I managed to hold it in.

'I can never resist one.' I didn't look him in the eye when I said it – it was too silly. He went with a small beer.

'I have to drive,' he sighed.

Little by little, we both relaxed and opened up. It was nice to have someone new to talk to. His main focus in life was his daughter, which I hugely envied. I wanted children. I think I wanted to make up for my mother somehow. I told him all about it. I never told people about it, about her. About what happened and how I felt about it all. How she never told my grandparents who my father was, how she had left a letter saying she was going and that was that. I told him how it broke my heart not to know more. He listened with a compassionate

44

ear about how all I knew of her was from photos and school-work books, and that she left with only the clothes on her back, and how my grandparents didn't speak of her much. It was always clear the pain she had left them in, and I always felt it would be selfish to make that worse. I had no idea if she was alive or dead, why she didn't take me with her, or if she ever regretted the decision.

'Regret seems unlikely though. I've lived in the same village my whole life. I wouldn't be hard to find,' I said.

In turn, he opened up to me. He explained that although he cared for his wife greatly, they married because she had fallen pregnant with Gaia. They had been friends since school, best friends. He wanted to do the right thing by his daughter and was continuing to do that every day.

'She was a Greek beauty, and I did love her. But mostly as Gaia's mother and a friend. That sounds awful... I've never said that out loud to anyone.'

'If it's how you felt, it's how you felt. It'd be nice if more people took responsibility for their children and loved them no matter what... Being a fantastic father isn't something to feel bad about...' I paused to consider my words carefully. 'Did you treat your wife well?'

'Of course. She was my best friend. I miss talking to her. I feel for her every day that she has missed watching Gaia grow.'

I was very curious about Gaia still. Gaia and her mysterious eyes. 'Why the name Gaia?'

'You have an obsession with names.' He didn't know it, but he touched on a nerve with accuracy. It hurt not knowing why or how my name was chosen. 'That was all Katerina. She was very into Ancient Greece and female strength and empowerment. She wanted a name to represent power for her

45

little girl. When she was pregnant, she would touch her belly and talk about how strong our little girl was, and she chose a name to make sure Gaia would always be reminded of that.'

I shivered at the memory of the girl, in spite of the warm night, so warm in fact that I could feel droplets of sweat at my hairline. That my hair was quite thick didn't help. I ran my fingers across it to distract me from my new-found goosebumps.

I said, 'It's getting late. I'd best call a taxi otherwise I'll never make it home!'

'I'll take you if you like.'

'Haven't you had a little too much to drink?'

'No,' he laughed. 'Look at me. I wish I were that much of a cheap date!'

We walked quietly along the main road. There was noise all around us from various bars, and people walking from place to place, but we were in a bubble of silence again, now more comfortable to be so. I could feel his eyes looking down at me as he opened the van door and held it as I got in. I gave him the address to put in his sat nav, and we were off.

'Thank you for a lovely birthday. I expected to be back home and asleep by now if I'm honest.' I wanted to look at him, to watch him, but staring at someone in a van was pretty obvious. Shame. The whole thing seemed to be a shame, it's not like it could go anywhere. I really liked him and I was quite sure he liked me too. We had loss in common, which was a funny place to start, but it strangely comforted me. Somehow he stopped me feeling like I was still hanging under the water in the middle of the night. It'd been a long time since I'd been attracted to someone, in part because I hadn't seen anyone in so long, or at least not without a mask on. Even when I'd actively looked, I'd never found anyone nice by using an app, so I just avoided trying. Then, where do you meet someone in your late twenties and early thirties? Apparently in another country, which is totally useless.

I was mildly tipsy still when the van stopped, so I asked him if he'd like a night-time walk on the beach. We took our shoes off at the door of my house and walked along the short dirt path until our feet hit the sand. He placed his hand on the small of my back, causing my spine to feel like a wobbly electric eel. We walked down to the sea with only the cushioning sounds of waves between us. He turned to face me, eyes reflecting the moonlight. He cupped my face with his free hand and kissed me gently, with soft full lips against mine. Calm washed over me. My heartbeat felt audible but not rushed anymore, and I was aware of everything in that brief and beautiful moment – the touch of the waves licking at my feet, the smell of seaweed and Anton's hot flesh, my hair moving across his fingers in the breeze, the fever from his hand moving across my spine, all of it imprinted itself on my mind. Everything.

I carefully pulled away, placed my hand on his prickly chin and smiled. 'Goodnight.' I walked away which was possibly the hardest thing I've ever done – to walk away from a compassionate, handsome Greek in paradise. I deserved a medal. I went into the house and shut the door. I stood leaning against it for the longest moment with the memory of him on my lips, with his handsome masculinity and tender kiss lingering in my mind. Damn my sensibilities and my morals. I wasn't the holiday romance type. I floated up the stairs and lay down on top of the bed, falling sound asleep in my clothes.

I awoke strangely content, and strangely early only to realise I looked like yesterday. I brushed my teeth and decided to go for an early morning swim before my shower. I slipped on my lime-green floral bikini, grabbed a towel and my phone and headed for the door. As I went to walk through the door, I went flying with a scream. I was sprawled on top of Anton with my legs in the air. I'd been looking at my phone and hadn't seen him there. If it hadn't hurt so much, I might have laughed.

'What the hell are you doing here? You bloody maniac! Seriously?' He easily looked as surprised as me. My eyebrows were almost in my hairline they were so high. His mouth was wide open and gulping air like a fish. 'Well!' I demanded. I'd managed to twist as I fell, which saved my knees, but left me with rather a painful hip, bottom and wrist. I was trying to scramble to my feet, cover myself with my towel and was secretly wishing I'd washed my face before my swim.

'I'm so sorry.' He was repeating it like a mantra at this point. 'I was putting my shoes on last night and just sat thinking, and I must have fallen asleep against the door. I'm not a maniac, I promise!'

'Don't be so ridiculous! How? Who would do that?'

'Me! I didn't mean to. At first I was hoping you'd come back, it was late, I was leaning on the door... I don't know... me. The answer is me.' He was clearly telling the truth. He was still on the floor looking completely bewildered like a toddler lost in a supermarket. I couldn't help it. I burst out laughing. Really laughing.

'You *are* a maniac!' I managed, through my tears of laughter. He still looked bewildered as he made it to his feet while rubbing his face.

'I really am sorry. Are you okay?'

'Well, my bum hurts fairly.' I'd pretty much stopped laughing,

48

but my side now hurt as well as my bottom.

'Let me have a look...'

'What? No!' I screeched and started laughing again.

'No, no I didn't mean like that! I just meant, I don't know, I just wanted to help.' He then followed this with some phrases in Greek, scruffing up his already mangled-looking hair and waving his arms about. At this, I wrapped my towel about my waist and started walking to the sea. I was still smiling to myself. It was not at all how I had anticipated starting the day, yet it was strangely fabulous. I had got to see his beautiful, rugged face once more. The strong, sweeping jawline, and bright eyes framed by thick black eyelashes. They were so wide that morning he may have been blinding the sun. I threw down my towel and started walking into the sea.

'Wait! You can't leave it like that!'

I kept walking, then as soon as it was deep enough, I was swimming. I could suddenly hear loud splashing noises behind me. I turned around to see Anton marching into the sea in just his pants. I couldn't believe it. I assumed he would just leave. What was there to say?

'What are you doing?' I shrieked at him. He dived into the shallow water and appeared, shimmering with droplets, in front of me. He stood looking down at me.

'Why are you walking away all the time?' His subtle little Greek accent popped out a little more in his passion. 'I thought you liked me.'

'It doesn't matter whether I like you or not. I'm here for a month! There's only one thing that can happen in a month and I don't need the complication!' Although I could do with the human contact, I thought.

'So, I'm just a complication? I tell you things, I share with you and I'm just a complication?' His heavy brows pulled down over his eyes and he shook his head. With a hard exhale, he turned and splashed his way through the sea with bounds and strides.

As I swam, I heard his van speed away. I stopped for a moment looking across at where it had been parked. The sea nudged at me, tormented me, prodding and poking. Was I foolish to let him leave? To not see where it could go? It was too late anyway. He had gone. I'd pushed him away. It was the smart choice. I hadn't put "meet a gorgeous man" on my Corfu to-do list, so it wasn't important. I repeated these thoughts to myself for the rest of the day. The whole time my chest felt tight and breathless. I needed a distraction, so I sent Maria a message on Facebook and arranged for her to stay over the following night. It gave me something else to focus on.

Chapter 7

I tried to do some work but I couldn't concentrate on it. Still desperate for distraction, I hired a car so I could explore a little. The island was so beautiful, lush and green with olive trees and fruit trees clustered about all over. I decided to drive to the Byzantine castle, Angelokastro, the castle of Angels, the highest point on the Corfu shore. I had never been before. We had always said we would, but my grandparents were elderly, so it didn't materialise. Mostly we enjoyed lazy beach days, good food and copious jugs of wine. It took me almost an hour of driving through the undulating terrain of green and gold. Seeing the odd village or hamlet, or even lonely home, gave my mind open space to ponder, daydreaming about who resided within those buildings, with no one else close for miles. How would it be to live in true solitude, not just the loneliness in my mind? It was all so tranquil – other than the momentary horror of passing a tourist bus near a sharp drop.

I parked and paid, then started making my way up the many, many steps. Each one was a tapestry of stones, some shaded by more olive trees, some golden and cooking in the sun. It wasn't long before I was fanning myself with my hands and huffing at the hot air. I stopped to rest near the top of the climb, next to a lizard on the white-grey stone. I took a photo across the expanse of green. Trees and hills covered the earth with a rich, deep green when looked at en masse.

My heart sat in my stomach from the moment I had started my ascent. I could see my grandparents in my mind's eye, younger than when I had lost them, Mama holding Papa's arm and telling him to slow down and appreciate the view. He would want to march forward and look at the details of the place. As a teen, I would trail behind them either laughing or rolling my eyes depending on my mood. Now, no matter how hard I tried, it wasn't real and I'd give anything just to roll my eyes at them one last time. I swallowed hard and pushed my feet firmly onto the grey stone to ground myself with every step.

There were parts of the castle that felt rather precarious, but it was worth clambering across prickly rocks in flip-flops. I sat at the top of a sheer drop, looking down on the shrubs and bushes managing to survive by poking out of white rocks. Then, next to the drop was the view across the sea – deep blues and turquoise as far as the eye could see. I sat ignoring passers-by and just watched the calm of sea, imagining a life that would never be lived, one with a family that wasn't real, that was mine.

The sun was almost unbearable. I could feel my skin being tortured by it. Rebelling against my urge to move, I punished myself, and absorbed the rays with zeal. Luckily, there was the odd slap of wind, which hit the sweat on my collarbone and forehead, making them momentarily cool.

What must he think of me? I couldn't help but indulge myself by thinking about Anton. The problem was, my feelings for him were terrifying me. Not just anything physical, that was a bonus. I'd never spoken to anyone about my mother in any detail. Certainly not how I felt about it all, about her. Even with long- term boyfriends I had kept details to a minimum. Maybe his role as primary carer for a child left him more open and caring, ready to look after people. Or perhaps it was just him.

Talking about my mother had torn at a wound I always tried my best to ignore, but one whose presence I was always aware of in the hollows of my subconscious, secretly affecting all the decisions of my life. She was the reason I had waited until university to lose my virginity. I was terrified of getting pregnant so young or with the wrong person, terrified I might turn into her and leave a helpless baby behind. I could never do that. When I eventually did take that step, I had been in a happy relationship for almost a year. Everyone I knew was having sex. I'd relaxed a lot since those days, but I was still one for relationships. There couldn't be a future with Anton, not so far from home. I had two homes back in England as it was, the one I had made for myself and one half a mile away that I'd grown up in and inherited. I couldn't easily leave all of that on a whim.

My legs began to go numb from sitting on the edge of the rock. I shifted, but I didn't get up. I took a bottle of suntan lotion out of my bag and added a little more to the high points of my face. As my hand glanced over my nose, the smell of the SPF30 liquid pulled a little smile from my lips. Something about it was as comforting as the smell of cinnamon-infused mulled wine at Christmas. It was ingrained in the magic of holidays and being around happiness and love.

I became aware of an American couple talking over me, taking photos of my view. They stood over my head talking about how frightening the drop looked. Before making my move, I scooped up a sharp little stone from the bleached dirt and dropped it over the edge. I watched it topple helplessly, bouncing over the shrubs and green, until eventually it was out of my sight – which was disappointing to me, as I wanted to see it dive to the depths of the water. The Americans gave a little gasp at my action. I got up before the heat killed me and to move away from their nattering above my flame-ridden skull.

I looked around some of the more interesting nooks and crannies of the fortress, but even with its broken, almost accidental beauty, my mind wasn't there with my body. It was lost looking in at itself. So, I made my way back towards the stairs, creeping along past the stacks of stones and photo-takers. I was almost at the point of descent when I caught my flip-flop on one of the ruins, making my foot shoot forwards, sharply slicing the tip of my toe on a rock. Blood started pouring out of my big toe.

'Shit! Shit! Shit!'

I was pretty sure this time Anton wouldn't appear to stop my tears and give me an oversized plaster. The warm liquid ran over my fingers as I desperately clutched my foot. A similar sensation hit my cheeks as tears fell across them. I had been ready to burst since the night before. Everything came crashing down on me. I did my best to keep it silent as I quickly hobbled towards the stairs leaving a trail that would've made Hansel and Gretel proud.

After twenty minutes of hobbling, I was back at the hire car, sat with my bum inside and my feet outside. I had a nice slice in the tip of my toe and I was beautifully covered in red-brown dried blood. I only had a small packet of tissues and some water to clean it all with. People along the way had offered help, but I had shied away, keeping my distance with strained smiles and watery eyes. It was times like this I would miss my grandparents scooping me up. But I didn't. I missed Anton.

Chapter 8

There was no warning, no knock at the door. She just marched in with ouzo in one hand and limoncello in the other. In Greece, no one locks the doors, and she knew I'd be no different.

'Well, *kalispera*, Maria.'

'*Kalispera!*'

'I hope you don't mind.' She had a giddy look about her and I could hear talking outside the door. Harry walked in, hands neatly in the pockets of his shorts.

'*Kalispera*, Melodie! This is Nico,' Harry said, and nodded towards a young man trailing behind him. He had shaggy brown hair, a slightly large nose and was very slim. He was attractive, with a cheeky half-smile and pretty-boy puppy eyes. My hand pressed against my face as I forced a smile though my fingers. This was in no way the night I had intended or planned for. I could feel high levels of awkward moments on the horizon. At least I could always depend on alcohol to help me through.

'Nice to meet you, Nico.' I smiled again but with my mouth,

not my eyes, and gave an awkward wave. To my side, I could see Maria's mischievous red lips displaying pride at her match-making. Her intention may have been sweet, but it was totally absurd. He was at least five years my junior, maybe more. Not that that would matter other than he looked like it too, younger in fact. He was such a baby face. Plus there was the same problem as with Ant – where could it go? Nowhere.

'How long are you on the island for?' At least I could enjoy his beautiful Greek accent. He gave a little eyebrow movement and curled the corner of his mouth. My stomach did a flip, not in the way he would've liked, I'm sure. More to create a burning acid sensation in the back of my throat.

'Around three more weeks. Can I offer you some wine or we now have ouzo and limoncello? I also have soft drinks.'

We all sat down outside with glasses of wine. There was a small round table with four chairs on a grassy area between the house and the sand. Maria was still smiling and I was already feeling irritated at the whole thing. I wanted to just say goodnight and walk away. Instead, true to my British ways, I put out a bowl of crisps and made polite conversation. That lasted around twenty minutes or so.

'Well, this just won't do!' Maria announced, then jumped up and ran into the house. She came back clutching the bottle of ouzo and shot glasses. 'Let's play a game! Who has a game?'

'Truth or shot?' said Harry, with a half-smirk as a cigarette hung out of the side of his mouth.

'Aw, just like old times, hey, Melo?' Maria wrinkled her button nose in my direction. 'Okay, so the rules are you either tell the truth or take a shot if you don't want to tell. Got it?' We all nodded as she filled our glasses. 'I'll start. Ask me anything!' We all paused to think, looking around blankly for inspiration.

Truth or shot holds more potency in high school or university when you might actually want to know silly details about each other. 'Come on, you lot!' Her smile had shrunk and she pulled at her tight skirt, shuffling in her chair. 'Anything! Come on! Please!'

'Okay, okay. How about, why are you marrying Harry?' I asked.

'Well, that's bloody easy. I love him. Always have. This game should be truth and shot. It'd be more interesting with questions like that! Melo, your turn.'

'Fine, ask away.' There was the pause again.

'Nico, don't you have anything to ask?' Maria was grinning at him and may as well have said "nudge-nudge, wink- wink". I couldn't look at him for fear of another come-on look. He muttered in Greek before going into English.

'Sure. Do you think I'm handsome?'

Brazen. I enjoyed that his "sure" sounded like "sore". It felt like a statement on the situation. I took the shot rather than stroke his ego, which just caused uproar and giggles, while I looked to the sky, wishing for the juxtaposition of Ant's touch, soft and strong, gentle but full of power. Why was I enduring this? Stop. Lighten up, I told myself and mentally rejoined the group.

'Your turn, Nico!' Maria was almost giddy. She slid her hand across the table to squeeze Harry's. If only she had known what I was really thinking.

'I have a question.' They turned to look at me, eyes wide. 'How old are you?'

Nico looked me square in the eyes and drank his shot. He kept looking at me as he spoke.

'Harry, how often are you have sex with Maria?'

Maria nearly spat wine over him then started to cough. He was still looking at me with little creases in the corner of his eyes. Perhaps he found it as awkward as I did. Maria hadn't taken her eyes off Harry, who was calmly filling the breeze with the smell of smoking.

'Now, it depends. We don't have set days or amounts. There's no average, but it last happened three days ago. Is that enough?'

Nico turned to look at Harry.

'Yeah.'

'Maybe we should play a different game,' Maria suggested, with a little urgency in her voice that made me want to laugh out loud.

'I don't know. I thought we were all starting to break the ice a little.' I found myself smiling towards Nico.

'Fine.' She grabbed the packet of cigarettes off the table and placed one between her slim, perfectly painted lips. Harry pulled the lighter from his shorts and threw it at her.

'Ask me anything,' she said out of the corner of her mouth.

'Is Harry the best you had?'

My head spun to look at Nico again; he was just toying with them now.

'Of course,' she said through a cloud of smoke. I was glad we were outside. 'With questions like this I'll never get my shot!'

Nico was looking at me, eyes following the lines of my floral dress. I picked up my wine, enjoying its earthy aroma and his attention.

He said, 'When did you last have sex?' He grabbed the cigarette packet from the table. Just me who no longer socially smoked, apparently. I kept sipping my wine, then looked at the lipstick-stained glass and the swirling red liquid.

'I honestly can't remember. It was with my ex, well in

59

advance of us actually breaking up. So, a couple of years, or more.'

They sat in silence looking at me. I should have taken the shot. My cheeks started to burn. I picked up my shot glass and downed the contents even though I'd told the truth.

'There's been a pandemic, you know. When did you last have sex?'

'Two weeks,' he said in a matter-of-fact tone.

I was being judged for my choices. I picked up the ouzo bottle and refilled my glass and took another shot.

'Figures. So, Harry, do you feel awkward right now?' I tugged at my dress and slapped my hands to my knees. He just took his shot. 'Maria, how about you? Awkward?' She took hers. 'Great, well you got to take your shots anyway. Please excuse me, I'm just going to pop to the loo.'

The plastic legs of my chair caught on the grass as I pushed it with the backs of my knees, making standing an embarrassing kerfuffle. I was then left with the challenge of trying not to look like I was storming off. My head felt a little cloudy from the mixture of wine, ouzo and annoyance.

I held the sink in the downstairs toilet and stared into the large, square mirror. I spoke to my reflection like I was my only friend.

'Calm down. Just enjoy yourself. Nothing matters. You have nothing to lose so nothing to worry about. No one to worry about.' I liked how I looked that night, at least. I always had time to spare, so wasted a fair amount on doing my makeup, something I usually couldn't be overly bothered with. I touched just under the neon-yellow eyeshadow that splayed out with a black, winged line below it. A bold mask, because why not? I looked down at my maxi dress, black with neon-yellow flowers, more camouflage. I was starting to regret the effort. Maybe I was silly. I had no grounding. I used to talk to Mama when I felt lost. She would always give me sound advice. She was compassionate but tough. There was comfort in my own face as it reflected hers so well. She had given me her high cheekbones, her big round eyes and even similar curved lips that curled up slightly at the edges. Our builds were quite different, though. I had always assumed my height was from my father's side. Not that I could ever confirm that, only Mama and Papa were on the short side of average. I was staring at the mirror, wishing the reflection would turn into Mama and say something useful, when a knock made me jump.

'Are you okay, girl? I'm sorry if it's all a bit much.'

I opened the door and leaned on the frame.

'Mmm. I forgive you.'

Maria wrapped her arms around my waist.

'I'm sorry, I thought making it like old times would be fun. I didn't realise you'd turned into a nun.' She squeezed me tighter.

'What do you mean? I'm the same girl I've always been, give or take a large percentage of grief.'

'No, you used to have fun with the boys.' She wasn't letting me go. I think she wanted to talk without looking me in my eyes.

'What do you think I was getting up to? I have never had sex on this island, I'll have you know.'

'Really?'

'Truly. No shot required here.'

'Okay, I'm sorry.' She laughed and let me go. I started to walk away from her.

'That doesn't mean I was a nun.' I turned to look at her,

poking out my tongue, and chuckled as I came out of the front door.

'Right. Shots all round. That's the bloody truth!' No one disputed me – they all took their shots and the glasses were refilled. 'New game! I Have Never.'

They all nodded and leaned in, waiting for me to start.

'I have never had sex on this island.'

They all drank and banged the glasses on the table when they were done. I pointed to Nico.

He said, 'I have never had sex in England.' The rest of us drank, and I pointed to Harry.

'I've never...' He hesitated, eyes darting. 'I have never had sex in the sea!'

Nico drank. I pointed to Maria.

'Never have I ever played this game before!'

We all drank; she was, of course, lying just to take another shot.

'Right then, ice is officially smashed and everyone is a little more caught up. Can we all be adults again?'

'I do not think I can.' Nico put his hand up like he was at school, which made me realise I was yet to sit back down.

'And why not?' I sounded like a schoolmarm.

'I am only twenty-three.'

After what felt like hours more of shots, I couldn't feel my toes. Which was nice for the one with a cut, but I knew it meant I was pretty drunk. Nico walked around the table and grabbed my hand.

'Let's go to the beach,' or *beetz*, as the alcohol made his accent more pronounced.

We left Maria and Harry having a little debate about guests at their wedding and how many they were allowed. We were stumbling along hand in hand, swinging them like children.

'You look eighteen not twenty-three, you know.'

'Oh yes? I hope I do, always.'

I was back at the shore, in the moonlight with a man, or perhaps a boy. He was very slight and only just taller than me. His T-shirt looked too big for him and I pulled at it absentmindedly as he faced me. I hadn't noticed how he was looking at me. I still had a laugh across my face at his boyish frame. He grabbed me and kissed me hard, groping at my arse like he was desperately searching for money in a back pocket. I didn't stop him – not at first. Then I managed to pull myself from his surprisingly firm grip.

'Look, you, I'm not that kind of girl. Didn't you get that from truth or shot?' I slurred my words a little, but at least they made sense. They even came out with an over-exaggerated shrug.

'We can still have fun.' He gently pulled me to him, this time by my protruding elbows. Apparently, I had left them accessible post-shrug. He kissed me again. I was finding it hard to contain a laugh. I had to stop him again.

'I'm sorry, Nico. You're a very arrogant little boy. You're nice too, but pretty bloody arrogant. Don't worry, you can still sleep in the spare room, that's where the arrogance can stay.'

I ran up the beach, my sides hurting from laughter. At least this time I was happy to leave a man standing there. I said goodnight to Maria and Harry on the way past and left them all to sort themselves out. I just wanted to sleep off the stupidity of the night.

By the time I woke up they had all gone. Maria had left me a note:

Thank you for inviting us (me) over. I promise next time it will just be me! Sorry about any mess. Speak to you soon. xx

I sat on the sofa more confused than ever, tightly gripping the scrap of paper. It's hard to make changes when your moral compass is dead. I imagined it was how Pinocchio felt when he lost his cricket. Suddenly you're just alone one day and you don't know how it came to be. Pushing away people who were kind might not be the way forward, though. Too late now – I had no way to find Anton. I shivered as the air con came on and tickled the hairs on my neck.

Chapter 9

I spent the next couple of days tanning and healing my wounds, which were both emotional and physical at that point. I had been in Corfu for almost two weeks and it had been a lot more eventful than I had intended. I was still unsure if it was exactly what I needed or if I should just go home early. To decide, I would drive the thirty minutes to Agios Stefanos that afternoon. If it soothed me, I would stay; if I felt like putting my head back under the water, I would go.

It was quiet walking along the main road. Mostly because it was early afternoon and tourists were eating or sheltering from the sun near the sea. I thought I would grab a milkshake to cool off – better than starting on the ouzo. On my way, I popped into one of the small supermarkets to pick up some little soaps and treats, just in case I did leave in the next few days. The smell inside was reminiscent of a greenhouse bursting with fresh fruit and veg that was being slightly steamed in the humidity. Picking up a basket, I hesitated in front of the shelves of gifts, spotting a stand with delicate bracelets and keyrings. It was pointless to stop, as I couldn't think of anyone to buy for. I moved along and stood mindlessly adding soap to my basket, when I heard Greek voices coming up next to me. I stepped out of the way with a glance, only to do a double take, twist around and knock over half of the soap collection with my basket. It was Gaia. She took one look at me and snapped into English. Like her father, she only had a hint of a Greek accent, and only on certain words. You would hardly be able to guess her mother tongue.

'Are you okay?' She seemed softer than before, and started grabbing at soaps with her friend to be helpful. I didn't answer her straight away, I just joined in with the game of catch the soap while staring at her. Getting my own back for her ogling on the plane.

'I'm okay. How are you, Gaia?' The words slowly escaped my lips.

She looked at me properly then smiled – not a big broad smile but a low one with quizzical eyes.

'It's you.' She went into Greek to her friend, who smiled at me and then left us alone amongst the soap.

'Which ones will you buy?' She pointed into my basket then snapped her eyes back to mine. She just seemed so intense.

'I'm not sure. My name's Melodie, by the way. I don't think I said before.'

'Nice to formally meet you.' She gave a wide smile, her straight teeth shining with a clear retainer.

'I think I'll just get these ones.' I said, indicating towards my basket. 'It was nice to see you again.'

'I'll walk with you.'

It was strange; what was with her and her father elbowing into my quiet life? I paid for the soap and she stood watching me, before starting to chat to the woman behind the counter in Greek. I just looked from one to the other, pressing my lips together into a smile.

'It was nice to see you again. Thanks for helping with the soap.'

'That's okay. Where are you going now?'

'Erm...' – I hesitated, unsure if I should say. 'Silver Star, for a milkshake.'

'Perfect. I need a drink.'

It suddenly dawned on me that she might know about my interactions with her father. A chill radiated around the back of my neck, piercing through the heat of the sun. My mind was playing in a loop while we walked along together in silence. I told myself to act my age and make conversation instead of replaying details of her father. She was, after all, only a thirteen-year-old girl.

'How's your father?'

'Odd. But I think most men are.'

'You're not wrong there,' I noted under my breath.

'So how come you're in Agios Stefanos? It's a bit touristy for a local girl, I'd have thought.'

'How do you know I don't live here?'

A shred of panic soaked into my mind. I needed a sensible explanation for how I knew she didn't actually live there. 'Well, most people don't live here, do they? I thought most people lived in a nearby village.'

'Yes. That is true. My best friend actually does live here, though. Her family have a taverna and sometimes I help with the washing-up to earn some money. My dad does work here too sometimes.'

'Oh, really? What does he do?' I hadn't spoken to Ant about work at all. I was intrigued. I'd been in his van, but it didn't offer an obvious job title or logo.

'Well, mostly he does whatever he wants.' She laughed. 'He and Mum did up properties in England and Corfu. Some to sell, some holiday homes. Dad gets bored so he helps with deliveries or acts as a local handyman. Nothing very special.'

'Do you live far from here, then?'

'Karousades. I don't suppose you know it. It's about thirty minutes in the car.'

I shook my head. At least now I knew roughly where he lived, which was only fair as he knew exactly where to find me.

The bar had stairs leading up onto a stone terrace, which over- looked the point where two roads met on a bend. It was fenced in with short pillars in a row, with a ledge running along – a fantastic vantage point for people-watching. I followed Gaia to a table at the front, next to the pillar wall under a large red umbrella. We both ordered strawberry milkshakes and she was back at it, looking at me, flattening her brows into slim lines, face squished as she leant on her hand. Even so, she was a very beautiful girl. Long thick, dark hair, her father's striking eyes and a delicate, almost turned-up version of his nose. Her mouth was unfamiliar, wider, perhaps, finer in the corners than Anton's, and holding more of a feminine, youthful pout. Perhaps like her mother's.

'I'm sorry if I'm bothering you, but I'm Greek and I remember names and faces. I feel like I should know you. I don't recognise your name. Your face I know! It's driving me mad.'

The mystery was solved. She'd likely seen me here before. I sat back in my chair and felt some of the tension lift from round my neck.

'I've been coming here on and off for years. You have

probably seen me around the resort when you were younger.'

'That can't be it. We only moved to this end of the island about six or eight months before lockdown. I've only been spending more time here this summer, helping my friend's family. Unless you also visit other parts of the island.'

'No – when we visit Corfu, we always come to Agios Stefanos.'

'Who's "we"?' she said, then leaned in to sip at her straw.

There are always those moments when you forget yourself, forget your loss. Perhaps thinking they're in the other room, getting a drink, or in the loo…but they're not. They're gone.

'Oh, I used to come with my grandparents. But they died.'

'I'm sorry about that. I understand loss. My mum died when I was three.'

I already knew, of course. I did not think that was the time to tell her I'd kissed her father and wanted him more than I wanted to breathe.

'That must have been really hard.'

'It was.'

Maybe that's why she seemed older and more confident than the average thirteen-year-old. Perhaps it had forced her to just grow up. I wondered if I'd ever find out the full story.

'I still need to work out how I could recognise your face so strongly.' She took a longer sip through her straw while watching my face.

I felt like I should pull some kind of awkward, silly expression, but I side-stepped the urge and just tilted my face.

'I wish I could help. I always thought I looked a lot like my grandmama. But she was much prettier than me.'

'Wow, then she must have been truly incredible or you're very modest.'

I looked down at my ring and twisted it between my fingers. 'Well, thank you. You're too kind.'

She was still intently watching me when her phone buzzed. She looked at it, quickly typed out a message and sent it. Then she was back to studying my face. Her phone buzzed again, and she repeated the actions, back to me and another message, reply and back to me.

'Anyone interesting?' I smiled. I wasn't used to hanging out with teenage girls. Not since I was one myself.

'Just my dad.'

Unfortunately, I had been taking a sip of milkshake. It caught in my throat and danced on my trachea, then across the table in an insane splutter and manic coughing.

'What on earth! Are you okay?' Just like her father before her, she jumped up, knocking her chair flying to come to stand next to my embarrassment. People often say 'I wish the ground would open and swallow me up'. There wasn't enough soil in the world to cover the glow of my cheeks.

'I'm fine.' My voice came out almost an octave lower than normal. I made a mental note to stop choking on my beverages and to generally drink more slowly. It would save my embarrassment and the planet in terms of napkin waste. 'Sorry. My drink went the wrong way.'

We were both wiping up my mess, and I was wiping my chin when I saw him walking towards the bar. He hadn't seen me, though. I had the rush of fight-or-flight adrenaline hot through my chest.

'I'm so sorry, I've got to go.' Groping into my purse, I threw down some money, grabbed my things and ran. I ran; like a fool, I ran. This particular bar had two entrances. One with stairs, next to where we sat, and a second at the side that came out at street level due to the undulations of the resort. He was nearer to the stairs entrance, as he was crossing the road from that direction. The other entrance meant going across the whole terrace to come out of the other side.

I stayed stooped over in an attempt not to be seen over the very low wall – the wall made of pillars with gaps between them. At least I was wearing shorts, not a skirt. As I stepped out, I did so right in front of Nico.

'Woah! Oh Melo, throwing yourself at me. I'm not surprised.' He pushed up his sunglasses onto the crown of his head to display his puppy eyes and gave his signature child-smile. I hoped that as I was facing Nico, Ant wouldn't notice me.

'Melodie?' No such luck. Needless to say, the pillars were my new enemy. Why did I suddenly think my life could move on from its normal farcical ways? I edged round to face him. Well, his chest, anyway.

'Anton.' I smiled but still didn't look further than the expanse of his chest. 'Nico, Ant, Ant, Nico.' The silence suddenly seemed very loud and it was like the world had stopped dead to stare at us, like a cheap sitcom, which wasn't all that funny. I could've guessed who would speak first.

'So, how do you know beautiful Melo?' Nico said. He threw one arm around my shoulders and gave a squeeze. He wasn't that much taller than me which made me feel like we were two naughty children looking up at our father. I quickly shrugged him off, but I was left with his woody scent lingering around my head.

'I don't really.' Anton said. That hurt. He was looking right at me too.

During our one evening together we had opened up. We had told each other so much. It had meant something. I didn't

71

know how to respond.

'Well, I – '

'It was nice to see you again.' His tone was flat. He attempted a smile but most of his face looked numb and didn't move. Assuming he wasn't coming from a Botox appointment, it was safe to say that was that. 'See you around, Nico.' Anton said with a nod. He walked off towards Gaia, who had watched the whole thing with her mouth half-open.

'Do you know each other?' I looked from Anton's back to Nico's arrogant face.

'Melo, it's a small tourist resort – What do you think?'

I started to scurry away, wishing myself to be as invisible as one of the stray cats; just part of the scenery.

'Going so soon?' Nico called in my wake.

I started marching while desperately trying to stop my flip-flops from loudly slapping the scorching pavement. I had to march past the front entrance. I stayed close to the wall so they probably couldn't see me. I was mortified by the whole experience. That was it – I hadn't gained the peace I had been looking for. I'd had enough. I was going home.

Chapter 10

I had managed to book another flight, but it didn't leave for a few days. There were still fewer people flying in the world, so fewer flights to hop on. I decided to spend the evening thrusting clothes into my suitcase while drinking limoncello on ice. I froze; I was sure I heard something. Then again, definitely a little knock. I twisted at my opal ring with my thumb as I crept down the stairs. The door wasn't locked; I had no real protection.

'Hello?' I called as I edged towards the door.

There was no answer. I pressed my back to the cool white wall, looking around for a weapon better than my phone.

'It's me, Anton.'

I was suddenly moving, darting around the room, a couple of paces in each direction like a caged predator. There was nothing to do but invite him in and calm down. Remember to sip drinks not spit drinks.

'Come in!'

The door opened and there he was. It felt like his only purpose in life was to make my heart feel like it was going to implode under its own weight. His stubble was a little more beard and his emerald eyes were just that: cold stones. He was looking through me.

'Gaia said these are yours.' He walked further into the room and carefully placed my sunglasses onto the coffee table. He turned to leave, but I couldn't let him go this time. I needed to know him more and I didn't care about logic.

'Wait, please. I can't stop thinking about you! Please!'

He turned to face me, but his stone eyes hadn't changed.

'I thought I was a complication.'

'You are.' Half of my mouth curled up. 'Apparently I'm drawn to complexity.' I shrugged a little, trying to seem cute and not tipsy from the limoncello.

'I have a daughter and I don't like you using us. I hadn't told her about our…whatever it was. After this afternoon, after you ran away from her, I had to tell her something. You ran away from her! I haven't told her about anyone I've seen since her mother died.' There was heat in his voice and his hands were the only part of him that was animated, going from tense and flat to giant fists.

I could feel my throat closing up. I wanted to let excuses overflow. I wanted to pour them out of me. Anything to get him to look at me the way he had before. I also wanted to know exactly how many women he had seen.

'She followed me to Silver Star. I didn't ask her… She's a credit to you by the way.'

'Do you know what the worst part is?' His heavy brows were drawn together.

I shook my head frightened to find out the answer.

'She liked you.'

I swallowed my urge to cry. I knew I had no right to cry. I

was wishing I hadn't drunk so much.

'I'm sorry. I like her too.' I hadn't thought I would. After the air had been cleared, she was quirky and charismatic. I could have easily spent the day in her company. 'Would you like a drink? I have limoncello, I think.'

He hesitated, got his phone out of his pocket, presumably to check the time, then looked back to me.

'Okay.'

As soon as he agreed, I darted towards the kitchen portion of the open-plan space. This had the advantage of being able to keep my eyes on him while I made his drink. I was afraid if I left the room, he would disappear and this would all be an alcohol-induced apparition.

'Here,' I said.

He had sat on one of the sofas. They were red, yellow and navy check dotted with round navy cushions. The one he sat on was large enough for me to sit next to him and still feel like I was giving him space. Like a kneading cat, I rubbed my fingers into the worn material.

He said, 'So, who's Nico to you?'

'Oh God! My friend Maria decided it would be a fun idea to attempt to set me up with him. He couldn't be more wrong for me.' I held my hand to my face in memory of the whole night and looked at him through my fingers.

'I think he likes you, you know.' At last his face broke into a smile over his drink – the first real expression since he had arrived.

'I think he likes any woman with a pulse!'

'You don't know how beautiful you are, do you?'

I was taken aback by this comment. Maybe I didn't. Like most women, I was highly self-critical: too thin, too fat, never just right. He just came out with it too. He had honesty in a way most people don't, because they're too guarded to release their feelings readily.

'I don't know...'

'You are the most alluring woman I've ever met. When I hit my head on you at the airport, you stunned me. Even with half your face covered. *Gamoto*,' he said under his breath and rubbed his beard, 'I haven't stopped thinking about you from then to now. And you're so clumsy! It makes me want to laugh at you and protect you, and even my daughter thinks you're beautiful and kind, if a little strange. Unique.' He wasn't looking at me, as though ranting to himself, or perhaps his glass. He drank its contents and placed it onto the table. 'I've got to go. I'd still like to know you more, even if it must be as friends.'

I was still a little stunned myself. I managed to nod and I think I managed to say yes.

'What's your number?' he asked.

I took his phone, put my number in it and rang my phone to check it and, of course, so I had his.

'There. Now you can find me when you like. I think you're beautiful too, you know. Inside and out.' My words were bashful, stupid, cliché and paled in the shadow of his, but they were true. I was clutching my knees; I was still in my denim shorts from the day. He stood up and stretched a hand towards me to help me up. I took it and he pulled me towards him. He kissed me. He kissed me harder than before and held me tighter. I clutched the sleeve of his shirt in one hand and the back of his neck with the other, running my fingers across the bottom of his hairline. A delightful shudder ran down my spine. He released me, and our faces hovered an inch or so from each other. I had been stretching on my tiptoes. I let my feet fall back to the ground. He looked me in the eyes as though he was searching for an answer, then gently leant forward and pressed his lips to mine once more. He started to walk towards the door.

'Oh, by the way, Gaia asked me to tell you, she remembered who it was.' And with that, he left.

Needless to say, I couldn't sleep. I might never sleep again. I sat up on the edge of the bed with the bedside lamp on. Venus was watching over me as I debated whether I should message him. No – I didn't want to seem desperate. The problem with that was I'd never felt this way before. I almost did feel desperate. Just desperate to run my fingers along the hairs on his forearm and up toward the back of his neck again. When I was around him my body was on fire and my soul froze still. Everything was in a muddle, calm but magnetic, determined but lost. I wanted to tell Mama the whole stupid story. I needed to tell someone. I wandered down the stairs and sat at the breakfast bar looking across to where we had sat. I ran my fingers through my hair then pulled it tight. I got up again and walked out of the front door. The sea was gently crashing on the sand. I sat down on the edge of the beach, toes touching crunchy seaweed. I inhaled the coarse, salty tang deep into my lungs. I sent him a simple message:

Thinking of you.

It was true, and I didn't feel like playing games. After ten minutes with no response, I told myself he was likely asleep. It was almost midnight after all. With no one around but the night sky, I got up, slipped off my nightie and walked into the sea. The cool water made me shudder, but it was what I needed to take the edge off the heat he'd left me with. I lay back and looked up at the stars, floating on the waves. The sound of a car door slamming woke me out of my trance. I stood up in the water; it only came up to my waist so I sank into it. The car was outside my house. I could see the lights. Suddenly I could hear my phone ringing. I just stood there in the water, unable to bring myself to move. In the peace of the night, I could hear footsteps cut through, crunching down the dirt path from the house to the seaweed. I could see his silhouette, instantly recognisable.

The thin moon shone brightly, as it so often does in a cloudless sky. He stood for a moment watching me. I was a little way out – it still wasn't very deep where I was stood. He pulled his shirt over his head in one easy movement to reveal his firm torso in the dim light. His chest was covered in a light smattering of hair. In a second swift move he was naked too and walking towards me with the confidence of a man who had every reason to hold his head up high. I saw his body tighten as the waves crept up his thighs. I hadn't made any intentional movements – I just bobbed about with my mouth agape. Occasionally, the sea seemed to nudge me in his direction. I didn't know what to think – one side of me wanted him to come over to me, hold me, take me. The other side was scandalised by the whole thing.

Neither of us said a word. He ran his wet fingers through my hair and across my jawline. He sank into the water to meet my eyes, carefully pulling me close, still eye to eye. Our wet bodies pressed together. I tentatively put my hands to his solid collarbone, tracing a line with my fingers to make sure he was real. Still no words had been spoken, but so much had been said. He moved in and kissed me, slowly, his warm mouth breathing life and heat into my body. His hands ran once more down my back, this time finding their way across my curves to lift me up into a delightful embrace, weightless in the hands of the sea. My fingers were running lines through his hair, my arms were about his neck.

Before our souls decided to dissolve further into the sea, he spoke.

'You're freezing.' Wrapping his arms firmly around me, holding our slippery bodies tightly together. 'We should go indoors.'

I nodded but still couldn't find words to say. I slid from his torso like silk on silk before we walked hand in hand towards the house, collecting our clothes on the way.

I leapt upstairs to grab some towels from the cupboard, pausing to look in the mirror and mouth "What on earth" at myself before running back down the creaky wooden stairs.

'Here you go, here you go, here you go!' I chanted as I threw the towel at him. My jaw was clenched and my arms were covered in goosebumps as the air conditioning came back on. Anton was suddenly shy. He was holding himself, as though he were in a line-up in front of a football goal. He, of course, had to let go to catch the towel. I watched him as he wrapped it about his waist.

'I have to say, I am pretty surprised to see you back here so soon,' I said, as I sat down in the middle of the stairs.

'It wasn't exactly planned. I got your message and, I don't know...' He walked over to the sofa and sat down.

I got up again and eagerly followed.

'I just got in my van and here I am. I should probably go.'

'No, stay!' I quickly lay my head on his lap and put my feet

79

up on the arm of the sofa. I was looking up at him, smiling, and he returned my contented expression with his own. He started to stroke my matted hair.

'What is it about you?' His voice was soft and low.

More like what was it about him?

His fingers traced the outline of my face and down my neck. He could probably feel the speed of my pulse.

'Would you like a coffee?'

We sat in our towels clutching our matching white coffee cups. He was still on the sofa and I parked myself on the floor on the other side of the coffee table, looking up at him.

'Gaia is beautiful. She's determined that I look like someone she knows.'

'I can't imagine there are two women as striking as you.'

I lifted an eyebrow at him over my cup.

'Really?'

'You own a mirror, yes?' He sent his eyebrows wiggling right back at me.

'Well, I'm glad you think so. I'm very intrigued as to who apparently looks like me though.'

'You'll have to ask her when you see her.'

My heart squeezed. What was this and where was it going? I would stay until my later flight, but that was still only around two weeks away. Perhaps it was not the time to over-think or worry about the future. If the pandemic had taught me one small thing, it was that life can change at a moment's notice, or with no notice at all.

'I shall, if I'm allowed to spend time with her.'

'It's funny, ten years since I lost my wife and I've only dated two women in that time. Gaia didn't know about either of them. I worried that it would hurt her. But she was pleased I was moving on. We spoke a lot this afternoon, when you left.'

'I bet she thought I was insane running away from her like that. I just panicked. I didn't want you thinking I was some bunny boiler talking to your daughter.'

'She was confused, but then just thought it was really funny. She told me about the soap too.' He leant his elbows on his knees and gave a low laugh.

'Well, I'm glad I'm a source of entertainment for you both.'

He was still chuckling to himself as he put his mug down.

'I don't know where this is going. I know you live in England. But is it okay if we don't think about that? You're the only woman I've opened up to in ten years. I can't explain why that might be, but I'm not willing to just ignore it.'

He got up and placed himself on the floor next to me, with long legs outstretched and resting on one muscular arm. The coffee table sat in the corner of a large navy blue, bobbly rug that he was lying on. I turned and instinctively kissed him. We slid down and lay next to each other in a warm embrace. It was very late, and I fell asleep in the comfort of his warm arms. I had never felt more safe, and less alone, in my life.

Chapter 11

I woke up with a start as Anton sat bolt upright.

'*Gamoto!*' He jumped up from our pile of white towels. 'What time is it?' He continued his rampage in Greek, while nearly falling over to put his pants and shorts on.

I groped around to find my phone.

'It's 9:34.'

He didn't answer me. He just grabbed at his things.

'Ant… Ant… Ant… ANTON!' He stopped and actually looked at me. 'Your shirt is inside out.'

He looked down bewildered and burst into laughter, rubbing his face.

'*Efcharistó.*' He came back to me, knelt down and kissed me. 'Tonight? Beachcombers? Eight? Do you want me to pick you up?' He was moving towards the door.

'Yes, please!' I called after him, and with a smile of beautifully straight teeth, he was gone. Like a dream or a distant memory. I lay back on the floor, holding our towels. They were still warm from our sleeping coil and smelt of him. I couldn't define the smell – it was unique, masculine, mixed with the fresh salt

82

of the sea. I stared at the ceiling for over an hour, recalling each moment I had been with him in a place somewhere between asleep and waking. I Pondered how he was confident and strong and gentle and unsure. I conjured his face in my mind's eye. Last night he had a scruffy beard and the hair on the very top of his head was all messy. It was endearing. I drew the lines of his warm eyes, tiny wrinkles at the corners, mostly when he smiled, and his strong, facial bones dulled down by his beard... to his wide, strong shoulders and beautifully toned torso, not overworked, and with a trail of hair drawing the eye down. I remembered the feel of his... My phone started to buzz. It was Anton:

Sorry I had to rush away, work. Gave Gaia your number. See you tonight.

I wondered why. It was nice that he trusted me though. The day went quicker than I'd expected, mostly absorbed in trying on every item of clothing as I unpacked my bag again. None of my underwear was overly attractive but luckily it was all just plain. I hadn't expected to have the requirement to worry about such things while I was in Corfu. In the end I went simple all over. A dress that was the colour of his eyes, and covered in large white spots. It had spaghetti straps with a straight neckline to it. A little white belt pulled at my waist and the fabric melted around my hips; short, but not too short. More that it was short because I was tall, not because it was designed that way. It was just enough to show off my long, tanned legs without the worry of embarrassment. I wore my squeaky stilettos and hoped that with different acoustics and flooring it wouldn't be such an issue. They were white and pointed. I hadn't worn them all that much before but they were my "lucky" shoes. Mama and I had been shopping in Cambridge, looking for something to wear to a wedding reception. We found the white shoes, but we weren't at all sure about them at first. In the end, they were all that looked good with the monochrome dress I'd picked out for the occasion. I found my last boyfriend at that wedding. I also wore them to meet an important Instagram client and to teach a seminar called "You and Your Social's Life", which gained me a lot of momentum in my career. Mama was the one who started to call them my lucky shoes. I couldn't not wear them. Even if they didn't feel very nice on my poor toe, the discomfort was worth it. I was hoping not to choke or fall into anything for a change.

I looked into the full-length mirror on the landing. I was sure Mama and Papa would approve, not only of my outfit, but also of Anton. They had always loved Greek people. The holiday appeal was not just the clear seas and delicious food – the people made it special. I could feel my eyes tingle and my nose wanted to run. I crunched my dress in my fists and hopped from foot to foot. It was no good, I had to tilt my head back and frantically wave my hands next to my face, then limbo my way to the bathroom in a dance to try not to let tears fall out of my eyes and ruin my makeup.

I wasn't improving my nervous energy by getting emotional. After carefully using a piece of toilet tissue in the corners of my eyes, I decided to distract myself with a jewellery change. From small earring studs to chunky white hoops and a matching bracelet, just playful enough to keep my mind from wandering back in their direction.

He arrived just after seven, this time in a yellow Ford

Mustang convertible.

'Gaia chose it,' he said, with hands up in surrender as though by opening my mouth I were holding a gun filled with words, I got in; the car was flashy for him, unexpected. 'I couldn't decide and I needed something to drive her around in when I didn't want to use the van. So, she chose this. It meant more to her than me.' He shrugged as he closed my door and walked around to get in.

'You're a fantastic father.'

'I love her. That's all I know. What's money for? Hmm?'

It was hard to talk during the journey with the top down but it was delightful to drive through the beauty of green Corfu, with olive trees rushing past us. He took my hand as he drove, and I felt like I was taking the power of the spinning earth into my bones.

When we arrived at Beachcombers, we were directed to the left. This was the corner with the enviable, uninterrupted view of the sunset. It was breathtaking, filling the sea and the sky with rich reds and vibrant orange. I had been there dozens of times before – it was one of many favourites. I'd watched the sunset countless times and from countless angles. With him it was different; it felt different. The sun was casting its enchanting glow on everything it touched. It touched Anton, it touched me. He sat next to me, not opposite, giving us both the fantastic view, although little elbow room. The sunset blazed across his eyes as he looked out to sea. My breath caught in my chest as champagne and olives arrived at our table.

'What's all this?' I said, looking between the waitress and Anton.

'I want to do this right. It's our first date. I want to show you how appealing life is.' He was calm, serious – his eyes didn't leave mine as he passed me my glass and made his toast. 'To beauty in everything, life-changing moments, and loud shoes.'

He made me smile at every turn. The champagne was perfectly cold against the warm sunset and the inferno in my chest.

'I may have a small agenda.' He raised an eyebrow as he carefully found a place for his glass on the little wooden table. 'Gaia wanted to meet us for drinks after our meal. Would that be okay? I dropped her off with her friends again. I can text her and let her know if not?'

'Of course! It'd be nice to see her.' Things were moving at a pace that made my head tumble like a dryer. This could at best be counted as a third date even though it was our first official one. It just so happened we had already innocently spent the night together naked. I watched him over my menu as I tried to choose between pork chops or curry. He had trimmed his beard back to neat stubble, which he gently scratched as he eyed his menu. The waitress came and went with our order as we made our way through the bitter-sweet flesh of the olives and sipped at our champagne.

'You fell asleep quickly last night.' He smiled at me as he tried to make himself comfortable in his chair. I was sitting with my knees away from him to give his long, hairy legs room under the table. Unfortunately, he made the chair look like one you might find in a primary school. Watching him made me shuffle around in my chair too.

'I did. Other than being extremely comfortable in your arms, I think we were perhaps going a little quickly and the emotion of it all tired me out.' Straight away I could see him hiding a laugh. His belly moving under his mint-green shirt. 'Are you laughing at me?'

'Maybe. In a nice way of course... It's only, if "emotion" tired you out...' His voice trailed off into his drink so all I could see were his jokey jiggling brows, then his shoulders joined in with his belly in their jostle.

The tips of my ears felt hot at his silly suggestion.

'Shut up, you arse, you know what I mean.' I rolled my eyes playfully then finished the contents of my glass as he let his laughter erupt through his chest and out of his mouth. I just kept giving him a sideways look, desperately trying not to join in with his hilarity. I couldn't really understand how he could find a laugh in absolutely nothing. But I liked it.

'Sorry, sorry.' He wiped a tear from his eye. 'I'm immature and you are beautiful. Ah! Saved by the food!'

The waitress carefully placed our plates down, bringing with her the aromatic spices of Anton's fish curry. Its creamy, golden texture made me a little envious, and I was tempted to ask if I could try some.

'Speaking of "immature"', I said, 'how old are you?'

'Why, do I look very old?'

'No.' He looked perfect. He had touches of dark grey in his stubble but otherwise his hair was dark, with no hints of age.

'I'm thirty-seven. Not too old for you, I hope?' He took a mouthful of his curry and watched me while he chewed.

'Sounds perfect to me.'

Our conversation was very different to our first. It wasn't the heavy exchange of storytelling or the download of our histories. It was more about light-hearted exchanges, people-watching – cat-watching, at one point – and gentle touches, fleeting kisses. We smiled for the sake of just being happy, now in the glow of a candle as we finished our champagne and left hand in hand, to meet Gaia.

I was apprehensive, but at least I no longer feared her intense looks. We met her at Athens Bar. We sat outside, again, to have the opportunity to converse while still absorbing the atmosphere, as the music filled the patio and laced the road outside. Anton made his way inside to order drinks and use the facilities.

I said, 'I'm so sorry I ran away from you! You must think I'm incredibly foolish. I panicked!' I was blushing at the memory of it and pressing on my cheeks with my fingers.

'Don't worry. My dad can be intimidating.' She laughed and I exhaled some of my tension.

'I just wanted to tell you who you look like! In case you have a long-lost cousin.'

I smiled at her, thinking how much she must love her father to want to make an excuse to get to know me more. She was sitting on the edge of her chair bouncing her legs inside her culottes.

'Go for it. Who do I look like? I hope it's not a reality TV person, because I won't know who they are.'

'No, no. She's here on the island. Her name is Lil. Lil Pellet, I think...'

She carried on talking. I couldn't tell you what else she said. Not a word, because the humid night held no mercy for me. All I remember was the heat rushing from my toes to my head in one prickling throb, and then I went blank.

Chapter 12

I opened my eyes to a blanket of faces. My focus was only on Anton. His hand was clammy on my face; I pressed mine on top of his. The night air was dense, oppressive on my chest, making it uncomfortable to breathe.

'*Kalispera*, handsome,' I said.

He muttered something in Greek, crossed himself, then scooped me up into his arms with ease. My eyes went in and out of kaleidoscope vision. I squeezed them tightly shut, and pressed my face into Anton's chest. The dull ache in my skull tapped away like a finger on a table. The people dispersed from around us, back to wherever they came from, chatting and asking if I was okay. Everyone was speculating as to the cause of my blackout, most saying it was the heat. Some mumbled that I needed feeding up. Anton took me to a different table, one to the side, and lay me on something that resembled a long sofa made of stone. The owner of the bar placed water on the table and spoke to Ant in Greek before leaving us.

'What happened?' I said, as I tried to focus my eyes. I was suddenly aware of Gaia at his elbow and it came back to me.

'You fainted. I think you hit the side of your head. Hit it on the ground.' His voice wasn't its usual low jovial notes; it was more uneven and rushed. His long fingers raced around my skull, searching. It reminded me of a time when my papa searched my scalp for nits. Just like Papa, Anton carried on until he had satisfied himself that all was well.

My squinting eyes fell on Gaia. The pair of them had matching frowns, only Gaia's eyes were glistening in the candlelight, and if she chewed her lip any harder, she would draw blood.

'Lil Pellet. Do you mean Liliana Pelletier?' My voice came out as almost a whisper.

Anton's head whipped round to face his daughter. I'd never said her name to him, but he had clearly put it all together. My mother. I hadn't said her name out loud in many years.

'Yeah, I think. Why? What is wrong?' She looked from me to her father, her gaze lingering on his face, desperately seeking his reassurance.

'It sounds like you might know my mother.'

'Oh,' she said, as she sat down opposite me.

I closed my eyes.

'I don't know her,' I said. 'She left me when I was a baby. That's why I was brought up by my grandparents.'

The finger-tapping in my skull had become a knocking fist that was hard to ignore. Anton was kneeling by my side, stroking my hand and looking at the floor.

'Hey, what's wrong with you? I'm the one who fell.' I attempted a laugh, but it hurt too much.

'I wasn't there when you needed me. I saw the whole thing and couldn't be there.'

'Yes, it's entirely your fault for needing the loo. I ban you

90

from all future toilet use.' I rolled my eyes and removed the cushion on the stone sofa to press my face against the cool grey rock. It was rough on my skin, like a pumice stone. It grounded me and gave a small amount of relief to my throbbing skull.

'I've never fainted before. I blame the champagne.'

'Champagne!' Gaia said. Her entire body language changed like the flick of a switch. She pulled her spine as straight as it would go, her fingers gripped the arms of the wicker chair and her eyes bulged out at her father. She couldn't contain a giddy little smile.

'And what's wrong with champagne?' Anton said in a low flat tone. His lips drawn into a line at her.

'Nothing,' she whispered, lowering her eyes to smile at her lap.

'So who? Where? Sorry. I just – I have a million questions and don't know where to start, I guess. Where do you know her from?'

'"Know her" is too much.' Gaia's voice was slow and the frown slowly returned to her face. 'A friend and I used to help people with fruit and olive picking, where we used to live. We were just bored and people let us, to feel helpful.'

Sitting up, even slowly, made my head feel so heavy I thought my neck might give way. I looked down at my "lucky" squeakers and knew Mama would have laughed at it all.

'Thank you, Gaia. I'm sorry, I've, yet again, embarrassed myself. Thank you. Thank you for telling me who I look like.' I wanted to reassure her. I tried to smile but even that hurt.

Anton reached out and touched the girl's cheek and tucked a loose strand of hair behind her ear. They were such a striking pair, with their golden-olive skin, brilliant eyes and matching high cheekbones. Gaia's hair was piled up high on her head in a way that was both neat and messy.

'Can we please leave? I don't feel at all well.'

Anton agreed and then started talking to Gaia in Greek. She was nodding with short replies. She got up, kissed me on the head, kissed Ant on the cheek, and ordered me to be better. Then she left before I could even scramble a reply.

'Where is she going?' I said, as I watched her go through squinted eyes.

'To her friend, Natalia. It's just around the corner, it's where she has been all day. Come on, let's get you home. I'm staying with you tonight. I hope you don't mind. I want to take you to hospital first. I worry you have a concussion.' He pressed the back of his hand to my forehead in that way that parents do to their children, as though they can gain vast catalogues of information with the back of their hand.

'I don't. I just have a headache. I'm not going to hospital. I'm fine. I fainted, it's hot, I need water and rest. But you are more than welcome to stay. Will you be sprinting out of the house again in the morning as entertainment?' I gave a small smile as he helped me to my feet and walked me out of the bar.

He looked down at me and gave me a squeeze.

'No, I'll stay as long as you need me. I'm also going to google signs of concussion.'

The air rushing past my face in the car helped with my head, and I started to see through the fog of my mind.

'I can't believe I fainted,' I said blankly, resting my head back to look at the stars above. They were bright and hypnotic, billions of wishes floating in the sky.

'You frightened the life from me.'

I enjoyed the little hints of Greek in his voice. He was drumming the steering wheel with his thumbs. He kept opening and closing his mouth as though he was going to say something but the drumming was bringing back the feeling of nausea.

'Could you please stop that?' I squinted in the direction of his fingers in the dark.

'Stop what?'

'You've stopped now. The tapping. I'm too sensitive right now.' I took a deep breath. 'What are you thinking? I feel like you want to say something.' I was rubbing my temples and I knew roughly what he was going to ask. I could hear him make a happy sound to acknowledge that I was indeed correct.

'Do you really think it's your mother?'

'I don't know.' I kept my answer short; I wasn't ready to over-think anything yet. I needed to lie down.

When we got back, he fussed around me. It was endearing to see this Hercules of a man cluck round like a mother hen. I guessed it was the role he was used to playing. It made me feel loved again, a sensation I thought had been taken from my future. His presence made my world full of possibilities. Perhaps it was my mother making anything seem possible? My mind was skipping like stones on the water.

'I've taken you up a glass of water and cup of coffee. You must lie down now.' I'd been sitting on the sofa watching him potter around. 'Is there anything else you need?' He leant over and stroked my face.

'No, thank you.' I started to climb the staircase with Ant following behind like the world's largest puppy. We arrived at the bedroom door, and as I looked in it dawned on me: this wasn't exactly how I'd thought the night would go. I hesitated before entering. Anton clearly picked up on my energy.

'Do you want me to stay in one of the spare rooms?'

'No!' I almost shouted and grabbed his shirt. We stood in the doorway holding each other. 'It's just – I don't know.' I looked up at him with my chin on his chest. His astounding eyes peered down at me with a smile in each corner.

'It's okay. I am here as your man-slave to keep you well!' The laugh that followed this statement rumbled in his chest, nearly jiggling my head off. It was not a way to cure a headache.

'Okay, man-slave, where is my shirt?'

'Shirt?'

'I didn't come to Corfu expecting man-slave company, you know. I'm usually a bit shy for all that. So, I only brought comfy, oversized, cotton nightshirts to sleep in.' I pushed my hand under the pale green pillow, and there it was, waiting to be found. I started to undress and realised Anton was just sitting on the bed watching me. 'Well, this seems a little unfair, man-slave.' I gave him a little nod and attempted to pull my face into a sad pout.

'Oh, yes, it is time to sleep.' He started to undo his shirt, but I was already down to underwear and, suddenly shy, was not really sure where to go from there. I turned around to remove my bra and put on my nightshirt. I was doing up my buttons as he was undoing his. 'That's not what I thought,' he said. 'How do you make a shirt look so…inviting?'

I gave a coy look from under my lashes, but I was fully aware I hadn't done up as many buttons as I normally would, in either direction, just the ones in the middle. 'Unfortunately, tonight you're not invited. Any sudden movements and my head might drop off.' I tried to laugh, but really, I was more than a little disappointed. Anton was now down to a pair of black boxers and disappointment shifted – only the headache mixed with longing was left. I stood to the right-hand side of the bed and peeled back the sheet to slip inside next to Anton. Luckily, there were no arguments as to who got which side as we curled up beside one another on the thin mattress. Facing one another, we were like teens at a sleepover, ready to gossip.

'What should I do? Should I find out if it is my mother? Gaia said she looks just like me. It can't really be anyone else. I can't imagine the name is all that common. What should I do?'

'I can't answer, Melodie-Mou. Only you can know.' He was right, of course; the "Mou" was new, though. 'The only thing I do know is, it's late, and I think you should sleep.'

He was right again. I'd ask about "Mou" in the morning. He kissed me and I didn't want it to stop. His soft full lips pressed against mine, lingering then gently kissing my bottom lip.

'*Kalinikta*, sleep well, and know that I am here.'

My body began to relax, leaving my mind to carry on whirling into sleep.

I rolled into Anton's back and sharply woke up. I wasn't used to sharing and that left me awake in the early hours. He was very lightly snoring with each breath. I traced his spine with my fingers, softly so as not to disturb him. It was all so surreal. After loneliness, boredom and devastation, I'd managed to throw myself into a parallel universe – one where I was happy, and I had the choice of confronting my mother. One where perhaps I could fill in gaps and understand why she didn't want me. I might even find out about my father. Maybe I would be able to meet him too – just to find out his name, what he looked like, if he knew I existed.

I turned onto my back, staring into the shadows of the room. My skin was cool from the air conditioning; it made my hot tears feel as though they might burn my skin like prickles of overflowing lava. I didn't mean to cry, but I couldn't contain it any more. I missed my grandparents more than ever. I didn't know it was possible. I could hear my papa say, "Come on, kiddo, it can't be all that bad", which he would always say when I cried. He would sit next to me, put his arm around my shoulder and squeeze. We were the same height, Papa and I. I always felt that I looked like a cuckoo in their nest. What would they say to finding her? We never discussed it. I don't think any of us believed we would ever see her again, not after so many years. My whole lifetime. They would never have wanted to be the ones to get my hopes up just to see them dashed. Had she been in Corfu this whole time? So close and yet so far? However many times I wiped my eyes, tears kept puddling out.

I was desperately trying to stay silent and still in the shadows of the bed, but I was finding my tears hard to contain. I decided to get up and creep to the bathroom. I ended up sitting on the floor, letting the emotions roll over me like a cascade of bricks. They hit me one by one: fear, loss, regret, hate, love, contempt, frustration, outrage…the bricks fell endlessly and so did my tears. I told myself I had to pull it together. I didn't want Anton to see me like that. Just a blithering mess.

I pressed a cold, wet flannel to my face and looked in the mirror. 'I feel like I know your face,' Gaia had said. I'd seen photos of my mother, of course; I knew she looked like my grandmother. Her hazel colouring was like mine too, although maybe she had grey hair now, or perhaps she dyed it. Aimlessly wondering, I rubbed the soft threads of my hair together. Wishing I could conjure her up with my mind. Different eyes, though, I recalled, dropping my hair. Hers were blue. I always wondered what colour my father's were. I wondered what she sounded like, what she smelt like, what clothes she might wear.

I had made my decision. I had to see her. I needed to talk to Gaia as soon as I could, so I could prepare myself. I went back to bed, cold but strong in my decision. I quietly slipped between the warm cotton sheets and wrapped my arm around Anton, melting into his heat for a few more hours of sleep.

Chapter 13

I rubbed my eyes, and the lids felt soft and puffy. I glanced about the room; there was no sign of Anton. I wondered if I had missed his skit that morning, although he had promised there wouldn't be one. I heard him downstairs, so I quickly jumped out of bed to wash my face and generally make myself more presentable. I sat back in bed waiting for his return while replying to work emails and posting on socials. I only had to work here and there to keep on top of things, which had made life more relaxed while being in Corfu.

'You're awake! *Kalo Mina!*' He was holding a tray with scrambled eggs and toast.

'Pinch, punch, first of the month and no returns!' I said.

We both laughed at our little exchange. I was just pleased to have correctly understood something outside of "hello" and "thank you".

'I made breakfast, although there was not much choice about what to make.' He looked a little disheartened, but I was still impressed.

'I think, because I eat alone, I don't really make much of an effort. If I bother with breakfast, I just have toast.'

We proceeded to organise ourselves within the sheets and ate breakfast while chatting.

'I've decided I want to see her,' I announced, before taking another mouthful.

Balancing food on the bed, emphasised Anton's size, making him look bulky and inelegant as he ate. Yet, even that somehow still made me glow from the inside out. It was that warmth you can only get from caring for someone and them reflecting it.

'Okay, so what next?' he said, tilting his head.

'I'd like to have a chat with Gaia, if you don't mind. I wouldn't have known any of this without her. She knows the most at this point.' I was eyeing his reaction but he was nodding the whole time, reassuring me.

'That makes sense. I'll text her. We can get her from Natalia's and you can speak at our house, if that's okay?'

'Perfect!'

'Speak for yourself.' He gave me a cheeky glance and placed his breakfast paraphernalia on the bedside cabinet. Passing him mine to join his, I rolled my eyes; in what world was I perfect? I lay down on the bed the wrong way round, pondering perfection. We were quietly smiling at each other. He ran his fingers along my thigh then pushed my hair from my eyes. I was still, leaning slightly on one arm, intently watching him watch me. His hand then moved from my face down my neck then between my breasts, where my top button was done up. With one hand he undid it, then followed with the others one by one. Carefully, he uncovered me and wrapped his arm around me, placing part of his weight on me, and kissed me. He turned his attention to my neck and I held him close, pushing my body against his. It only took the loud ringing of Anton's phone to cause us to jump apart like teenagers. Anton answered it.

I quickly grabbed some baggy denim shorts and a plain white top and went to the shower to cool off. When I got back, he was dressed and off the phone.

'That was Gaia. We should probably leave soon to pick her up.'

We got ourselves ready and left the house to begin my journey towards finding my mother.

Anton, Gaia and I arrived in Karousades. It was a beautiful area, and it made me feel bad for never properly exploring the island before. It was vibrant and green, with twisting tree trunks birthing fruits and beauty. Dusty roads with mysterious lanes led to more rugged scenes of nature – layered against stunning views across the vast sea from a high vantage point.

'Instead of going home, shall we go to Taste Me?' Anton glanced at Gaia in the mirror.

'I knew you'd want to show Melodie there,' she laughed.

With the convertible's top down, it was a slightly shouted conversation, but every interaction between the pair made me smile. They were full of in-jokes and phrases you only form with people when you spend real time together. It was a beautiful thing to see in a father and daughter. If anything, I was envious, and hopeful that that might soon be me with my father.

We parked directly outside the restaurant and I followed Gaia to a table under a vine-filled pergola, overlooking a vast expanse of trees and green. Many of the trees bore fruit, including one full of oranges growing up on the slope below our feet.

It was so beautiful and strange to have my feet in line with the top of a tree. Being high up on a slope gave the most enchanting views over the sea. Gaia told me that the view was over Astrakeri, where I was staying. It was only a ten-minute drive. Anton came back with menus for us to peruse. It must have been just past midday, or somewhere thereabouts. We all chose different toasted sandwiches, and as he went to order them I turned to Gaia.

'I'm not putting you in an awkward position, am I? Wanting to know everything you know? Plus having your dad look after me...' I put my hands on my face to hide behind.

'It's fine. I've had him to myself for ten years. He deserves to have a life too. I'd like to be able to leave home one day, free of guilt...' She paused, looking at her hands. 'Your mum was always nice to us. I sent my friend Anna a message last night. She was the girl I picked fruit with. She still helps your mum out.'

Every time she said "mum" it was like a shard of glass quietly cutting my flesh, so clean it's invisible until the blood pours out. I sat silently, glad I had my sunglasses on as my eyes started to sting.

'She would bring us drinks and talk to us. I only helped her out a handful of times. We didn't do big business or anything. It was something to do in the summer when we had nothing much else to do. We helped a small group of different people, and she was one. Honestly, I think she was lonely.' She was lonely. The words rolled around in my mind. She was lonely. She deserved to be lonely. The anger swelled up in my belly. I twisted my ring around my finger, trying to pull some strength

101

from the memory of my grandparents. Luckily, Anton came back from chatting to the man behind the bar.

'They'll bring it over soon.' His voice calmed me, but only a little.

'Do you know her address?' I managed to keep a tone as breezy as Anton's, but I didn't feel it. My stomach felt as tight as my clenched fists under the table.

'That was one of the reasons I messaged my friend.' She picked her little orange backpack up off the floor and pulled out a piece of folded paper. 'That's her address. I wasn't sure – I knew where she lived from memory, but I didn't know the address. My friend knew, though.' It was pushed towards me like a loaded gun. To me that's what it was. A loaded gun. Full of anger and hope, answers and questions. Our toasties arrived as Anton squeezed my knee.

'If you want me to come with you I will,' he said. It was a kind offer, of course, but not one I could take up. I needed to go alone. We all sat quietly, talking only now and then while we ate. I started to learn more about them. Their relationship was very mature – playful banter, love and respect all muddled together. I had never seen myself with a man who had children, let alone a widower with a thirteen-year-old daughter. The pair of them had brought so much intense emotional upheaval into my life. They were something I had never expected and could never have anticipated. The whole trip had taken a ridiculous turn that only fate could have seen. Mama used to always say, 'The most ridiculous stories are always the true ones.' I was starting to think she had been right. I tried to suppress the reality that I would have to go back to England. I would eventually have to sort through Mama and Papa's things and put my life in some kind of order. But in that moment I inhaled their light conversation, the delicious ice cream we ordered as a dessert, the close air and the stunning view.

Anton and Gaia took me back to their home. It was outside the main village, tucked away off the main road a little way along a dusty track lined with dry grass. It was huge. I'd had no idea. Beautiful stone walls with dark pink window frames and front door to match, with a bougainvillea archway. I'd always delighted in seeing the beautiful pink bougainvillea flowers when abroad.

'Wow, was it pink when you bought it?' I grinned at Anton. 'That's why we bought it,' he laughed and so did Gaia. I could see her smug look as we got out of the car. He clearly let her have things the way she wanted: the car, the house. It was no problem to me. I didn't even know if I was a fixture for longer than my trip – perhaps less than two weeks. It wasn't as though she came across as spoilt or anything like that, even though it seemed like she was. She always seemed very grounded.

The interior was light – airy with simple lines in amongst more stone. It was open-plan with a wall in the centre, which had a wide staircase leading up in two directions. To one side of the large wall was a beautiful wood burner facing the living area; the other side had a small loo. We walked towards the long brown leather sofas.

'I'm going to go to my room, if that's okay?' Gaia pointed at the wooden staircase and then took them two at a time when Anton nodded.

'Your house is incredible.' It really was, from the coffee table – which was basically just a boulder with glass on top – to the sepia family photo with his late wife holding Gaia. She was pretty. Not in the way I expected; I couldn't remember what I had expected. But she wasn't it. Short pixie-cut hair and a smile that mirrored Gaia's wide lips. The whole house was fascinating.

'A few years ago, I thought we must make a fresh start and, eventually, we found this. We wanted to stay in Corfu but didn't actually care where we ended up; it was about the right property to make a new home.'

'Gaia mentioned you had done some property development?'

He sat down in a beautiful brown leather armchair across from me. It looked delightfully soft as he sat, absentmindedly rubbing the leather arms with his fingertips. 'Did she?' A smile crossed his lips. 'Katerina and I developed places here for rentals and flipped a couple in the UK. When she died, I couldn't bear to do it alone. I tried to continue; I finished the ones we had started. It was something that was ours – I did all the fixing and design, and she did budgets and found the right places to develop. I still have the rentals here on the island and one in the UK.'

'Wow. Well, this place is stunning. I'm stunned.' I waved my hands at it all; it seemed too beautiful to be just for him and her. Maybe I was being sexist, but I hadn't thought this would be how a man and a child would live.

'Do you mind if I quickly shower and change? I'm still in last night's clothes.' He looked down as though that was horrendous, but he looked perfectly fine; it's not as though he was sweating in a suit and tie.

'Of course it's fine!'

He jumped out of his chair and jogged towards the stairs. 'Great. Help yourself to anything!' He ran up the steps just as Gaia had, only leaping three at a time. I scanned the room, the dark blue patterned rug, the large abstract painting behind the sofa. The styling was distinctive and masculine, a big contrast to the pink and white exterior. I got up and walked towards the back of the house. Past the photo of Anton and Katerina holding the adorable baby Gaia, past the wood burner, past the heavy furnishings. There was the kitchen; it went along most of the back wall. I was more interested in finding the garden and finding the view. I went out of the door to the right of the kitchen. It was just as I had anticipated: a wide garden dotted with fruit trees. There was a mosaic patio of reds and blues with a matching mosaic table and eight metal chairs. I chose not to sit there, instead walking deeper into the garden and selecting the shelter of a lemon tree. I pulled a lemon from a low-hanging branch before sitting down. I rolled the leathery fruit in between my hands. A friend at university had told me that was how to loosen the fibres of the fruit inside, ready to get the juice out. I held it under my nose for a moment. I pressed my thumbnail into its flesh until a fizz of mist burst out. I licked the sweetest sour juice from my thumb. The acid sat on the tip of my tongue, tingling and nibbling. I was tempted to go back for more of a taste, but thought better of it. Instead, I squeezed more juice on to my hands and ruffled it though my hair. It was the sort of thing I would do as a child in an attempt to lighten it, before I was allowed to bleach it or do what I wanted with it without asking Mama first.

I had put my mother's address in my pocket in an attempt to lessen its importance. Carefully tugging it from its hiding place, I sat and stared at it. As though if I looked for long enough, she would appear. I thought perhaps I would ask Anton to take me back to my Airbnb. I would need to prepare myself; but, equally, I wanted to see her soon or I might lose my momentum. Tomorrow, I thought. It had to be. Even in the shade it was clammy at this time of day. The heat was almost unbearable, but I didn't really mind. The dappled light through the tree was calming, like a child's night light. I inhaled deep breaths of the thick lemony air to fill my lungs with something other than fear.

'Hey you, I thought you had left!' Anton appeared, walking towards my resting place. 'Are you okay?' He squatted in front of me with a gentle frown on his face. Reaching out, I touched one bushy brow and then across his firm cheekbone.

'I'm fine,' I said, 'but I think I should go, if you don't mind taking me? I have a lot to think about.'

That night was the first one I'd spent alone in the house for two nights. I missed Anton's warm body next to mine. His size made me feel protected and, in that moment, I needed that. The sensible part of me knew it was much better to be alone. If he had stayed, only his body would have been on my mind and I had a million questions to ask my mother. Although, in reality, they all boiled down to one: why? Why did she leave? Why didn't she return? Why did she live in Corfu? Why? It dawned on me that she might shut the door in my face. She didn't want me as a baby so perhaps she wouldn't care to answer as an adult. I needed to get some rest but my mind was a blur of questions. I had even started to panic about what outfit I should wear; what most reflected finding a long-lost mother who didn't want me? As though it mattered. I had parents who loved me – they just happened to be my grandparents. They brought me up to be their world; I was cherished every single day. I didn't need this woman's approval. So why did I crave it, just a little? Eventually I drifted off into a dream-laden sleep, full of giant question marks and dragons eating white buildings with blue window frames and doors – none of which had numbers; they all had question marks.

Eventually my alarm woke me. I got washed. I got dressed. I did my hair. I did my makeup. It was time to leave. At this point I just sat in the Honda hire car. Just sat there. The engine wasn't even running, so I was starting to boil myself. I got back out, feeling my lungs cave in. I pressed my hand on the metal hood of the car and snapped it away as it was already too hot. After taking several deep breaths in an attempt to calm myself, I went back into the house and caught myself in the mirror. She looked like me. I was on this planet and it was her fault I was here. Looking down at myself, at my white kaftan, which apparently was the chosen outfit to meet a biological parent who had no interest in you, I spoke aloud, 'You can do this, you need to do this.' Making eye contact with the face in the mirror one last time, I got into the car and left.

Anton and Gaia had previously lived in an area called Kokkini. It was almost an hour's drive from where I was staying. I put the radio on with extreme volume the whole way. Luckily, her house was very easy to find. The satnav had taken me right to her door. I parked in the dusty driveway and slowly got out. I felt like suddenly I was the only source of noise. I could hear my heart beating in my ears, my footsteps crunch on the dry dirt, my shallow breaths. I stood in front of the little blue door – how could something so small, so simple, so in need of attention intimidate me so? I wanted to step towards it, to knock. Unfortunately, my feet were glued to the ground beneath them. I started to turn faint again.

Chapter 14

'*Yassou?*' A voice came from behind me and I instinctively screamed, jumped into the air and snapped around all at once. It was her. It was like looking in a mirror but with a few small wrinkles, lightened hair and a good few inches shorter. It was clearly her. She stood stock still as though staring at a ghost. Which I guess I was. A ghost from her past. One she most likely never thought to see in the flesh after thirty-one years.

'I'm—' I started but was soon interrupted.

'Melodie. My Melodie.' Her eyes were as wide and as blue as the ocean.

'Yes, I suppose that's correct. I heard you were here, on the island, and I just wanted to know why you left me?' Everything was coming out a little monotone and clipped in an attempt to suppress the quiver I could feel building in my voice.

'Left you?' Her voice was quiet and engulfed by the hum of the day. Her head shaking, her face creased, forming a particularly deep crease between her brows and along her forehead. There was a thick white scar running from her eyebrow into her hairline that formed a cross with her wrinkle.

Quite a mark.

She walked around me at a distance, as though I were some kind of predatory cat and she was my prey trying to sneak away without my knowing. She didn't take her eyes off me until she was safely in front of her door. We were standing looking at each other, breath and pulse elevated like we had just gone for a brisk walk. I didn't know if I should ask my question again or just wait. Her mouth started to open; was she going to defend her choices? I should just leave, was all I could think. Then she spoke.

'But I didn't. I didn't. I didn't leave.' With this announcement she slowly turned, walked through the tatty little door straight into a miniature of a living room and sat down, leaving the door wide open for all to see.

'I think perhaps you should come in,' she said. Her eyes gave away nothing more than surprise; I couldn't identify any other emotion. Unaided by the fact my brain was whizzing around in circles like a stupid Scalextric car. I stepped forward into her doorway. It was just as hot in her house as it was outside – perhaps more humid in than out. At least outside had a breeze. Watching her stare into oblivion was making my toes curl in my flip-flops. She stared at oblivion as I stared at her. Perhaps oblivion was staring at me and we were in a stand-off. I wouldn't have been surprised.

Eventually she turned her attention back to me. I must have been a silhouette to her, in her dark little doorway with the sun behind me. She clearly didn't want this, didn't want me there, didn't want my questions. I couldn't take the waiting around any more. I began to step backwards back into the light and towards the car. She leapt up and lunged at me.

'Please, please sit down!' My feet had a mind of their own,

doing as they were told, following her back into her home. It was stuffy and tatty; all of the furniture looked well-worn and nothing matched; likely second- or third-hand. There were no knick-knacks or paintings, only functional items. 'Would you like a drink?' she asked politely as though I was an expected acquaintance.

'No thank you. Only answers,' I snapped as she pointed me in the direction of an old armchair. I swiftly sat down and started twisting my opal ring. She looked not just like me, but like Mama and Papa. It was as though they were sitting either side of her, looking back at me. My throat felt so tight.

'Well, in that case, the answer is: I didn't. I didn't leave you. I would never have left you.' Her eyes were welling up, but tears didn't fall. Mine rolled back into my head.

'Well, that's interesting. Where have you been for the past thirty-one years?' I wrinkled my nose, irritated with her nonsense. Shifting uncomfortably in her chair, she physically withdrew further from me like a tick burrowing deeper into skin.

'It's not as easy or as simple as you're making out.'

'Well, can you explain to me, please? You say you didn't leave me – well, I don't remember seeing you every day growing up, or at my birthday parties or at Christmas! So, where were you? Why did you go?' My emotions were escaping me – I could feel them disappearing, evaporating into the heat of the room.

'I– I– I just – I don't think it's important. What's important is you. I can't believe you're here. Here in Corfu, in my home. It's been so long I'd started to fear I dreamt you.' There was a flutter of a smile on her face. 'I know you want more from me. I'm sorry I can't give it. But you must believe me – I didn't leave you.'

'Tell me why, then.' Each time I pleaded there was a small...
twitch, almost, like someone prodding her lightly in the ribs.
An unconscious tick? I had come for answers but, other than
confirming she was in fact my mother, I was more confused
than ever.

She started shaking her head again.

'Please, please let me get to know you. Let's forget about the
past, just for a moment and just be us, here, now. Please?' A
tear started rolling down her cheek with a thousand unsaid
words.

A large portion of my soul wanted to wrap my arms about
her and the other part wanted to shake the truth out of her.
I decided just to agree, to nod my head, to just follow the
unknown path with no expectations. Nodding was about all I
could manage. Apparently, expectations were indeed pointless,
as none of this was what I had thought. There was silence
hovering over us, sitting on top of the sticky air.

'I don't know if you realise,' she began, 'but it's exactly thirty-
one years ago today since I last saw you.'

My head shook slowly in a daze. I'd never known the exact
date, only that I had been a matter of days old.

'Well, it is. It's not something I would ever forget. I was just
now coming back from laying flowers behind the house when
I heard your car, and came to see who was here. I always lay
out flowers on your birthday and the last day I held you.'

She seemed so genuine. There was pain in her voice and
across the lines in her forehead. Baffled. I was baffled by
her. I started to really look at her, beyond her similarities
to Mama and me. I studied her drab clothes: a plain baggy,
old looking t-shirt and baggy, equally old blue linen trousers.

They were scuffed and dusty across the shins and knees. She looked rather dowdy, to say the least.

'What made you find me? How long have you been looking?' Her eyes sparkled amongst the gloom and her weight shifted in my direction.

'It was just chance. I don't think it should be my job to chase you.' My tone was unintentionally harsh but it was possibly the coldest thing in Corfu. Her lips pulled tightly together and I recognised the face of shame; it mimicked that of my papa if he were in trouble with Mama. A thin line not to be crossed; clearly, she didn't like being called out either. She did start nodding, though.

'Yes, that's fair enough. How did you come across me, then?'

'I've been spending time with a man, here in Corfu…his daughter felt like she knew my face; turns out it was your face. She used to help you with your fruit trees before she moved, apparently.'

'Gaia? I knew she had moved away. Wow, I saw her father once when he picked her up. He is huge!'

I couldn't help but release a small laugh.

'He is, yeah, but he is a bit of a gentle giant.'

'I'm sure he would be very lucky to have you,' she said, and my smile mixed with a frown; how would she know?

'How are my mum and dad? I think about them all the time.'

'They're – they're dead. They both died recently, during the main wave of the pandemic. Grandmama first then Grandpapa soon after; I think of grief.' There was no other way than to just come out with it. To me I was telling a stranger; to her, they were still her parents. She was quiet but she swallowed hard, almost audibly. She rubbed her fingers around her throat.

'I'm sorry to hear that.'

'I'm sorry to say it.'

'Please, tell me about your life, about who you are.'

There wasn't anything much to tell, not in my opinion, and I felt increasingly awkward pretending to be normal with her. I hoped that if I gave her a little of what she wanted, perhaps she would do the same for me.

'Well, I work in social media, helping people develop their platforms...' I found myself stuttering, lost for interesting words. My mind was as empty as her living room.

'Do you enjoy your work? Does it make you happy?'

'I guess so. I'm pretty good at it. I advise people on what to post on socials and when, plus I make some people's content sometimes. But mostly I boost people's posts and such. It's boring to most people, I'm sure, but I like the analytics of it all. Assessing people's behaviour and trends.' I was assessing her behaviour as best I could. I was better with the online mathematics of human behaviour; I wasn't so used to the face-to-face emotions of it all anymore.

'I'm sorry, but I think I need to leave.' I stood up and turned to go, desperate to vacate the steam room she called a home.

'You'll come back, won't you?' Her voice was pleading as she clopped along in her Crocs.

'I don't know.'

'Please. I want to know you. Please don't judge what you can't understand.'

'You're not letting me try to understand! This is all a little too much, pretending to be normal. I need to leave.'

So I did. I got into the car and left.

Chapter 15

I drove straight back to Anton's house and found myself banging on his door, not knocking.

'Woah!' The door swung open and I charged in, sitting down on his sofa.

'Well, that was pointless, wasn't it?'

'Calm down, Melodie-Mou. Tell me what happened.' He sat me down and held both of my hands. I wasn't sure if it was to calm me or to make sure I didn't hit anything beyond his front door.

'She was talking nonsense. Utter rubbish!' Gaia was peering down the stairs. 'Sorry, Gaia. Sorry.'

Her mouth was open and she was clinging onto the railing. She came creeping down.

'It didn't go well?'

'No. I didn't gain any answers. She seemed bloody deranged to me. Saying she didn't leave me. Well then, where was she? Urgh!' My hands pressed my face, pulled through my hair, gripped my knees. I wanted to start hitting inanimate objects again but I knew it wouldn't help and I'd just be embarrassing

114

myself if I did. Gaia was frowning, creating a small indent between her neat little brows.

'What is it, Gaia?'

'I'm surprised. She was just always so nice. Sorry.'

'What did she mean, she didn't leave you?' Anton piped in.

'God alone knows. I most certainly don't. She seemed genuinely happy to see me. I guess that's a positive. But I needed to leave. I couldn't relax feeling like I was being lied to.' I pressed my face into my hands and kept them there.

'Do you think you'll go back? And see her again?' Anton said. He was frowning too, matching Gaia's little indent with his own. They looked like beautifully sculpted bookends.

'I don't know. I need to clear my mind of it all. I'm really sorry to just turn up banging on the door. But I only have you two to talk to about it all. I haven't told anyone else.'

'It's all right. It must be very difficult. I can't begin to imagine.' He peeled a hand from my face and began to rub between my fingers. 'We were just about to make gyros. Let's sit down, the three of us, to take your mind off it.'

'Sounds good.' I managed a smile, for him.

Gaia got us all freshly squeezed juice from the orange trees in their garden while Anton finished putting together the gyros in the kitchen. It felt like a lifetime since I had been so well looked after.

When the house was overflowing with the tempting smells of cooking meat, sweet onions and peppers, we all sat down together. More and more it was like I was stepping into their family. It was comfortable. Too comfortable. Too easy. How could I feel like this with perfect strangers and yet I couldn't sit down and talk to my biological mother? The day was draining the life from my bones.

115

'Tell us more about meeting your mother, and what she said to you. You said she was happy? She always seemed very kind and quiet.' Gaia was a typical young teen in many ways: confident, inquisitive and vibrant. I wondered what her mum was like and what she would have said about me.

'She was happy, I think. But she was completely closed in. She just didn't want to have a real conversation. Or at least not about the past.'

'But you'll go back?' She placed her drink down on its coaster; the noise of glass on glass clanging together made me flinch.

'I don't know.'

'I think you should.'

'Gaia!' Anton narrowed his eyes at her and gripped his fork. She may have been overstepping, pushing me perhaps, but I was interested in her opinion and I couldn't feel annoyed at her interest. The poor girl's eyes darted between us, torn between saying what she wanted and the potential scolding that may come as a result. I pulled at the hem of my kaftan and gave her a nod to continue.

'Well, okay, I know it's different...my mum died and yours left, but if I could, I would see my mum. I'd do anything to know her, to ask questions. Even silly things, I don't know, like, maybe who was her first boyfriend? Or if she was the same as me with her opinions. I'd want to know if we could be friends or if we are like each other. It is so sad your mother ran away but maybe you will get to learn why. If you take time?' Her lips pulled tight into a wide smile, eyes still darting like a squirrel from Anton to me. Poor girl.

'Okay,' I said and placed my knife and fork down and leant my chin on my fist. I knew considering her words was an important step. I wanted her to know I valued her opinion.

'I think that's a good point,' I said. 'Maybe I am being too negative about it all. It's just hard not to be. I just miss being able to ask my grandmama and grandpapa about what I should do. They're my real parents, to me. Are you close with your grandparents?'

'Yes. We had been visiting the English ones when we met you. We see them as much as we can and talk each week. I'm also very close with my Greek ones. They're quite near to your mum. I see them all the time.'

'That's lovely.'

'They're very kind people,' Anton interjected, 'they've helped a lot over the years.'

Although I was smiling on the out- side, internally their presence made me nervous. I couldn't help but analyse every possible hurdle we might have to consider. How would they feel about Gaia having a stepmother if we did continue down this path?

'You're very lucky to have such a loving family around you.'

'I am, and if your mum could be someone for you, why let the past hold you back?' Anton looked up from his lunch with wide eyes again. I did my best to keep up my serene expression.

'You're painfully right again, Gaia,' I said with a curl of my mouth and a little puff of a laugh. She looked very pleased, her big green eyes shining with pride. Anton was smiling in my direction too. I think maybe he looked impressed, or pleased that I didn't dismiss her. The decision had been made for me by a wise old teenage girl. It was somewhat nice not to use my brain power to figure it out myself.

'Now that's decided, is it okay if we change the subject? I like your top, Gaia. Where did you get it from?'

It was a pale pink sleeveless shirt which tied up at the front. Her hair was loose around her shoulders that day. 'Stunning' didn't really cut it. She was looking down, pulling at it, smiling and chewing.

'*Efcharistó*! I got it when we were in England. My granny took me online shopping.' She laughed and wrinkled her lightly freckled nose. I understood, of course. 'They got me lots of cool things. Would you like to see?'

My eyebrows went up and I hesitated. I was taken back by how receptive Gaia was to me. I looked over at Anton, who was clearing away the little square lunch plates.

'You girls go have fun,' he said, and didn't even look up. Half his mouth curled up as he offered a last glance in our direction before striding back towards the kitchen.

Clearly pink was a favourite. Her walls were a soft pastel pink that she had paired with light moss -green furnishings. For a thirteen-year-old, her taste was exceptionally grown-up and elegant. I picked up a small iridescent vase and rolled its smooth surface around my fingers, just to carefully put it down again and move on to looking at the next well-placed object. I was quite envious and in awe of how beautifully put together it was.

'Did you choose your own decor?'

'Yep. Dad says I've got my mum's style. But he is pretty good too. He says he knows because of her.'

'Well, you're both better than me. My place isn't exactly… interesting. It's quite plain, really.' My mind started to wander to Anton's bedroom, imagining what it might be like. Gaia had sat on a fluffy, green stool in front of a dressing table. She wasn't saying anything but she was shifting her weight and she hadn't got anything out to show me.

'Are you okay?' I sat down on the edge of the bed opposite her.

'Can we talk?'

'Of course!' My pulse went up, anticipating that so far everything had been an act and now she would tell me to leave her and Anton alone. I inhaled deeply to settle my mind. The sweet scents of jasmine and fresh linens comforted my fearful heart.

'Can you not tell my dad?' Then it became a test. One of trust and loyalty. Perhaps one to test my viability in the household. My stomach tightened with a new knot. My fingers closed around a soft synthetic throw as I began to nod.

'Promise?', she said

'Of course.' I agreed because I had to, not because I wanted to.

'I've been dating this boy, Finn. My dad doesn't like him, but he doesn't like any boys for me.'

'Okay.' I wasn't surprised. Having a thirteen-year-old daughter that looked like Gaia, and no mother for guidance, must have been terribly difficult. She was already starting to shed the androgynous body of childhood. Coupling that with her bright eyes and the endearing look of a woodland creature was a marriage made in hell for a parent of a teen.

'He just turned fifteen but I'll be fourteen in a month so the gap seems bigger. I know with Dad that will not help. My question is, how do I know he is real with me? You and Dad haven't known each other long – how do you know he likes you? For you, and not' —she paused here, for longer than I would have liked— 'anything else?'

My mouth hung open for a split second as I considered how on earth I could go on to say something meaningful. I wasn't qualified to say anything meaningful. Honoured to be asked, terrified at getting the answer wrong.

'Well…' I followed this with a cliché throat-clear 'It might sound a little obvious, but I think the first point is to never feel pressured. With anything, not just…physical stuff, but pressured to change who you are in any way. A good person will always embrace who you are. Does that make sense?' My palms were sweating; I could feel the moisture on my knees as I rested my hands on them.

'Yeah.' Her hands tucked under her legs, watching her knees more than looking at me. 'Why do you like Dad?'

I had not been well enough prepared for the day. I held my breath before I began.

'He seems to me to be a good man. I like that he looks after you, and seems to put you first. I guess, with my parent issues, that's something I respect. He makes me feel looked after too. He has made me laugh, mostly by being a bit of a giggler – I'm not imagining that, am I?' She shook her head and laughed. 'Not to mention he is rather easy on the eyes.' I pulled my shoulders into a little shrug, desperate not to blush or show my nerves.

'He deserves to be happy,' she said. 'He has seemed happy. Not that normally he is sad or anything! He has just been making more silly jokes – giggling! You make him happy.'

Gaia didn't look at me with this comment; instead she spun around to look into her mirror. She started brushing imaginary knots from her silky hair and I gained a knot in my stomach. There was no way I could tell her if I was intending to be a permanent fixture or not. Perhaps I was wrong, but to me that was what she really wanted to feel out. Would I be staying? She was testing me out as a potential mother figure in her life. It had been just over two weeks. My heart was squeezing tightly in my chest. This felt worse than seeing my crazy mother.

'He makes me happy too. I know this isn't exactly how he would have had things. Bringing you into our relationship when we don't even know where it's going...'

'I think it's a good thing,' she said. 'He treats me like a child much too much. Telling me who I can and can't see.' She placed her brush down and looked at me through the reflection. 'At least I had spoken to you before I knew his interest in you. I thought you seemed nice then. You got me a milkshake even though I was being a pest.' Her broad smile lit up the oval in front of me. It would be impossible not to smile back at her – she was too much like Anton, with his fiercely dark brown hair framing her delicate rosy cheeks.

'Please don't tell my dad about any of this. He really doesn't like Finn.'

'Okay. Well then, it's only fair that it's my turn to ask questions. Why do you like Finn, and what makes you ask me for my advice?'

She slowly turned to face me again, eyes hidden under her thick black lashes. She balanced her elbows on her knees and her chin on her hands.

'Finn is cute. But he is also smart. We both like watching old sci-fi films too. I go to his and we watch films together. My dad would flip out if he knew we were in his room. My dad says he trusts me; I know he would get mad. Finn broke up with me for a little time, and he told me it was because he was frightened of Dad.'

'Your dad wouldn't really do anything, though, would he?'

'No, no, no, but his size makes him...you know?'

121

'Intimidating?'

'Yes! Plus when he wants to, he gets loud. It's the Greek in him, sounding like he is in an argument even when he isn't.' She contorted her face into a wide grimace, then let out a little giggle. 'Don't get me wrong, we Greeks are all the same really.'

'I can understand why it might put off some boys. But, if they like you, and they have good intentions, I don't think it'll prevent the right boy.'

'I think you are right... I had best show you some things Granny got me, otherwise I'll feel like I've lied to Dad.' As she rummaged through one of the drawers in her cupboard, I thought how impressed I was. She didn't want to be lying to him even if she wanted to keep her private life private. There were times she must have missed having a woman to talk to. I was lucky to have had Mama. Maybe if I saw Liliana again I could find out who my father was, and maybe get to know him too.

Gaia began to show me an array of clothes, accessories and makeup. She seemed to relish showing me what her British grandparents had treated her to. We were in deep conversation about shopping in Corfu town, when Anton knocked at the door and entered simultaneously.

'*Kalispera*, you two!' The poor man even had to duck through every doorway in his own home. No wonder the downstairs was all open-plan – it must have been tiring to continuously remember to dodge your own walls.

'I was getting lonely downstairs. I thought you two were never coming back!' His eyes creased in the corners and his cheekbones were higher than normal on his face. He must have been ignoring the fact my home was almost two thousand miles away. I tried to push the thought away too. I wanted to absorb them and dream a little. Everything Corfu was bringing me was a surprise, and at that moment I didn't want to overthink or question things. I had no energy left for it. So, I didn't.

I stayed for the rest of the day, spending time in their garden, hearing anecdotes of Gaia's childhood and Anton's mishaps. Learning how Gaia decided she wanted to cook all their meals when she was only five years old, to Anton's dismay. He made sure they only had salad for a week. That was until she got very upset at the whole thing, and he let her boil an egg and make some rock cakes for school. Which, apparently, he used to like to make with his English nan. Gaia took pride in telling me about a time when there was a big family do, both sets of grandparents and aunts and uncles all there for her birthday. At only six, she took herself off to the shops to buy more ice as they had run out. When Anton couldn't find her, he was apparently pulling his hair out, ready to call the police. She had come strolling in with a big grin on her face. Watching her tell the tale of triumph, laughing, looking at her father roll his eyes, just seemed to sum them up. She was seeking equality; he was horrified and a little bewildered. Their tales all boiled down to muddling through, bound together with love and laughter.

In the evening, Anton made us all moussaka and we sat outside drinking wine – fresh juice for Gaia. Eventually it was just the two of us, alone. Getting to know more about Gaia had been much better than I could have hoped but it was also nice to have Anton to myself.

'Gaia is such an intelligent and mature girl.'

'She does worry me. I would say growing up too fast, but it's too late for that...' He paused, sloping his head slightly. 'Have you ever thought about having children?'

I gulped my wine a little too hard, the painful ball of liquid pushed against the walls of my throat trying to escape. But it couldn't, and neither could I.

'Well, I've never been with the right person to make it a viable option.'

'Did you want children?'

Perhaps this was his way of weeding me out of his life if the answer wasn't suitable.

I gave a coy nod over my glass followed by a snippet of a smile. 'Would that be a problem?' This time, gulping my wine back was on purpose.

'No.' His answer was clean-cut. He wasn't looking at me any more, though, just gazing at the beauty of his own garden. 'It's a five-bedroom house – it could do with filling.'

I could see his ribs begin to jiggle.

'I think I would be happy with just the one, to be honest. One good one. One like Gaia,' I said.

His belly joined in the little bouncing. I don't know why but I found it strange for such a big man to be such a giggler over nothing. I liked it. 'Why are you laughing?'

'Because for a hypothetical conversation this is very loaded, Melodie-Mou.' He wasn't wrong. I was numbing the weight of the conversation by letting him top up my wine glass. But all I let out was a hum of agreement. I couldn't remember having this conversation with any other man. He was already a father. He was good at it too. He was able to give time and security. According to Gaia, perhaps too much time.

'I take it from the amount of wine you've drunk you're staying?'

'I could get a taxi. It's only ten minutes away.'

'No, I'd like you to stay.'

'I'll stay in a spare room, in that case. I think it's important Gaia doesn't think we are rushing anything. I don't want her getting the wrong idea.'

His lips fell serious for a moment, and he had one slightly raised eyebrow.

'That's what I was going to say. What made you say it?'

The wine churned in my overfull belly and I was wishing she hadn't chosen me to confide in.

'She's almost fourteen. I don't want her to think it's okay for a woman to devalue herself.'

'So that's how you see it?' He had a fitted white t-shirt on with an artistic outline of a face on it. The face was starting to have a mind of its own, dancing as amusement bubbled over him.

'Don't get me wrong, I'm live and let live. Thing is, I grew up knowing my mother had got herself into trouble at sixteen. Plus being brought up by an older generation. I think that all culminated in a slightly more traditional or old-fashioned view.'

'So, no sex before marriage, then?' His firm torso was jiggling more, and more; the poor line face couldn't control itself.

'And what if it were? Should I leave now?' I did my best to stay as serious as possible.

Slowly, his head edged round until he was looking me in the eye.

'You're thirty-one – surely you have?' His eyes were glinting, with a giggle behind them, but he had become determined to control it until he could be sure he was safe to let it escape. The burgundy drawing was momentarily still as he clearly held his breath beneath.

125

'So?' By this point I was also holding in a laugh, but I was determined to do my very best angry look.

'Oh.' He took the bait and there was an edge of panic. He sat up straight, running his fingers along his jaw then tugging at one fat little earlobe. 'I had no idea. I mean, after the episode on the beach, and I did feel like we were heading in a direction the other morning...' His voice was low and his cheeks were pink.

I was like a balloon ready to pop with helium giggles. It happened. I popped. Doubled over, my hair swayed from my tipsy laughter as I took hysterical gulps of sweet fruit-filled air.

'No – it might have been a while, but no, I'm not a virgin!' Tears were starting to fall with laughter. Not that it was all that funny in reality; it just tickled me to wind up Anton.

He picked up his glass and finished the contents.

In no time at all it was past midnight and we were still chatting in the garden, trying to minimise mosquito bites with yellow and green citronella candles the size of fireworks, that Anton had thrust into pots.

'I'm pretty drunk! I think you should show me to my room.' I slurred just a little.

'This way, my Melodie-Mou.' He did a small bow towards the door, but I was frowning, hands pressed to my hips.

'I am not a cow!'

He was still laughing as he showed me up the stairs to a large magnolia room with yellow accents and sunflower bedding. It had its own en suite with yellow towels and floor mats.

'Thank you. Good night, Anton.' I gave him a lingering kiss while the alcohol in me decided to squeeze anything I could grab. Stepping back, I didn't lose his eye contact as I closed the door. I'd never felt so smug.

I'd started to get myself ready for bed when there was a light knocking. My feet decided to do an over-exaggerated creeping across the floor before opening the door. It was Anton.

'And how may I help you?'

'Can I come in so I don't have to whisper?'

I swung open the door and stood back, carefully closing it behind him.

'I brought you these,' he said, passing me a toothbrush, toothpaste and one of his shirts. 'I know you usually sleep in a shirt; it will probably be huge on you but it's the smallest I have.' He looked very pleased with himself, rubbing his stubbly chin and showing me a glancing flash of creamy white teeth.

'Aww, that's so thoughtful. Thank you!' Drunk me was a lot more confident than sober me. As is true of every person I've ever known to drink. This was a problem, as holding Anton's attention, the fact he had any interest in me, was already giving me a big head. I took my kaftan over my big head, slipped off my underwear and stood for a moment in front of him before carefully placing on the shirt. Casually I walked towards him; he hadn't moved a muscle. At least, not obviously. 'Goodnight,' I whispered into his ear. I kissed his cheek and ushered him out of the door.

Chapter 16

Feeling rather heavy-headed, I left Anton's straight after coffee and three glasses of water. After a quick stop at my Airbnb, I was off, ready to try again with my mother. I arrived at Liliana's ready to be open, but apparently the door wasn't so ready. I knocked and knocked, but got no answer. I took a walk around her small, white, boxy house. I called as I went but she was nowhere to be found. Even though it probably wasn't locked, I didn't want to go in. She might think I was poking about. I sat on her doorstep tanning for the best part of an hour before deciding the car was a more sensible option for waiting; at least then there was air conditioning. Boredom and late nights kicked in, and I fell sound asleep in a matter of minutes.

A nail tapped on my window making me jolt, accidentally beeping my horn, which in turn made my mother jump. She seemed amused as I stepped out, holding my chest and gulping air.

'Sorry to frighten you. I'm just so pleased you're back!' Her enthusiasm was quietly comforting.

'You can thank Gaia.' I followed her towards her front door and back inside the house-cum-oven.

'I shall! She's got a good head on her that one. How long have you been waiting outside?'

I looked at my phone. It was almost half past three.

'Wow. I got here close to eleven!'

'I'm so sorry! I've been at work.' She put her finger in her mouth and bit at the nail; all of her nails were short or bitten — it was a habit I had myself as a child, but I had stopped long ago. Her hands weren't like mine at all, they looked rough and hard. Thick stubby little fingers as opposed to my well-manicured, pampered- looking ones.

'Where do you work?' I said.

'Just at the local supermarket, nothing special.' Her ponytail joyfully swayed as she walked towards the kitchen, dancing to its own beat.

'I don't know,' I said. 'During the pandemic supermarket workers were praised as heroes.'

'I didn't feel like work was risking my life. Not that I cared either way. I was just pleased to still have a job; tourism's the main income here, and some people were living on the breadline. The Greeks are amazing, everyone just helped everyone. They made it through together.' Her absent-minded wisp of a smile was so like Papa I'm sure my eyes popped out of my skull a little bit. 'Would you like a drink?'

'Just water please.'

She scurried off to the kitchen, followed by her dancing hair, leaving me pondering over how normal and everyday the conversation was — evidence that Gaia could have been right. Why let the past hold us back? I just had to suppress my questions and see where things would go.

129

I sat scanning the room for details instead. Usually, when left alone in a room, photographs or ornaments keep you company. They distract the mind and give an insight into someone's life. All I had to look at were very lonely items: old armchairs, a dark wooden sideboard, a fold-up dining table, and a nest of three small brown tables. I'd assessed the whole room in less than ten seconds but I'd gained nothing. At best I could say she was either low on money or didn't care much for things. It was stark with off-white, peeling walls, which could have made the room feel brighter, but instead it was just dark and desolate.

When she came back into the room, I was thankful to see ice in the water; without it I might have cried. She was muttering something I didn't catch and went back to the kitchen. I sat on the edge of the chair, straining to hear her soft voice and trying to work out if she was talking to me or herself. In a moment she was marching purposefully back with a tray of olives and crisps.

'You can't have had any lunch.'

She was so softly spoken at times and her round eyes were almost as soft.

'Fantastic, thank you.'

She carefully placed the tray on the nest of tables by my side and I gladly took some olives to suppress the edge of nausea and headache looming over me.

'Thank you for coming back. It really does mean the world to me.'

'I'm hoping we could get to know each other. You seemed to want to know more about me and I guess I'd like the same. If that's possible.'

She gave a couple of sharp nods, bouncing her hair.

'Like, how long have you lived in this house for example?'

'Almost fourteen years now I think.'

She had actually answered a question; I could barely believe it.

'Wow, that's quite some time. How come you don't have any photos or things out?'

She shifted in her chair, put her water on the stone floor, and she looked like someone was poking her ribs again by the way her body winced.

'I don't have anything to put out.'

'Fourteen years and you don't have one photo or anything?'

'No, I hadn't really thought about it to be honest.'

I didn't press the matter but it sat in the back of my mind mulling. How could that be possible? That was until I recalled my own isolation from society. Perhaps I was more like her than I had first thought.

'Oh well, very...minimalist.' I lifted my cheekbones in lieu of a proper smile. I'd unwittingly caused another wave of awkwardness between us. It was bad enough I was subtly hiding olive stones in my pocket because I didn't know what to do with them and I felt too silly to ask; I didn't need further cold moments in a hot room. All I could think was: Think! Think, think, think! Think of anything to say!

'Perhaps I could take a photo with you? To put up?' I said.

The apples of her cheeks saturated in pink and her eyes lit up as she nodded. I picked my phone out from amongst the olive stones in my pocket, and crouched next to her chair to take one of us together. I was looking at the camera, she was looking at me.

'Do you have a printer?' I asked while studying the image on my phone. Her expression was unique, hard to decipher. It

131

looked like a mixture of contentment, maybe love and possibly confusion.

'No.' Disappointment soaked her voice and her face crumpled into lines, like those of a discarded tissue.

'It's okay, I'm sure Anton has one at his, if not he would know someone who does. I'll get it printed for you.'

'That would be truly wonderful, thank you.'

'I guess I should get going. When is a good time to come back?'

'Not tomorrow, I have work again. How about the day after that? Would you like to have dinner with me?'

'I would love that,' I said, and I wasn't lying. I liked to look at her face and see my grandparents smiling back at me. She was my connection to them if nothing else and that was something I was starting to enjoy.

I went back to my Airbnb to have a moment to myself, a moment to reflect. I came to Corfu to find the memory of my grandparents and I had done exactly that, just not in the way I had expected. It was a rather serendipitous mess. But perhaps life was coming together in a way I could never have dreamt? My phone buzzed, nudging me out of my brain and back into the room. It was Anton:

Kali! How did today go? Any better? A x

I replied within seconds:

Kalispera! Much better thanks. Do you want to come over? Please bring food. :)

Within thirty minutes he had arrived and was cooking up a

storm in my kitchen.

'Where's Gaia tonight?'

'Seeing her friends Natalia and Nefeli.'

I wondered if that was really where she was, or if she was with that Finn boy.

'Everything okay?'

My head snapped up to face his words. My skin was suddenly tingling. I'd promised Gaia I'd keep my mouth shut about Finn but Anton's eyes were narrow and those brows felt like they were judging me. Unfortunately for me, my own eyebrows had likely given me away, frowning at my own thoughts.

'Yes, I'm fine, I'm fine. Just thinking about today. Do you have a printer?'

'I do. Why?'

I passed him my phone with the picture in question. 'Wow, your first photo with your mum? I think I have some photo paper, I'll print you some.'

'Perfect, thank you. Do you know where I could buy a frame in the morning? I want to frame it for her. She has nothing at all on display in her house. I don't want the first thing to be a frameless photo.'

'The small supermarkets have things like that but they can be a little touristy. You might be in luck.'

'It's worth a try!' I said with a shrug.

I enjoyed Anton's company even when we weren't saying much at all. I enjoyed looking at him too, his long muscular arms made me want to curl up close to him and never come out from his warmth – even on a hot day. He was wearing a fitted white t-shirt with navy shorts — nothing special, but on him they became something to revere. Watching his muscles move through the white cotton, not muscle-bound, no, just naturally well formed, or at least that's how he came across. His bulky frame was delicately adding pinches of herbs to our dinner through long slender fingers. I needed to stop lusting for a moment. It wasn't helpful to the logical lists I needed to run in my mind. Could I live in Corfu? Could I come here to get to know my mother and see where things would go with Anton? Of course his fitted t-shirt was in the "pro" column.

'Gaia asked me why I like you the other day.' She hadn't said I couldn't tell him that.

'Did she?' He turned from his cooking, eyes agog and biting his lip with a naughty little smile. 'What did you say?'

'I said I'd seen you naked and that was enough!'

Mr Giggler was giggling again, it really didn't take much to set him off.

'I hope you didn't!'

'No of course I didn't!'

'Well, I'm intrigued...' He paused, frozen mid-motion waiting for a sensible response, I supposed.

'I don't know, she put me on the spot. I said something about how I respect what a great father you are and how you look after me too. Then I said the naked thing.'

'Well, that seems fair enough then.'

'So, has she asked you why you like me?'

'No, but I think it's pretty obvious.'

'Oh?'

'I've seen you naked too!'

he said and I pursed my lips and gave a sarcastic laugh in return.

'What would you really say?'

He was pottering all about the kitchen starting to dish up a delicious-smelling meat in a sauce, something I didn't know, but couldn't wait to try.

'Well, I think I'd say…' Then he proceeded to continue in Greek, starting off with a laugh as I threw my head back in a joking frustration but then he changed as he spoke, the muscles in his face changed. They became softer, with no sign of laughter, he picked my hand up from the counter and kissed it lightly.

'Well?'

'Yes?'

'What did you say?'

'You know, you look good naked.' He said with a shrug. Turning away his shoulders were giving away his laughter yet again. I picked up a cloth napkin and threw it at him making him laugh out loud.

'I'm sorry, don't hurt me!' He put his hands up in faux surrender.

'Silly bloody man!'

'Okay, well, I'd say to her that it started with looks and intrigue as these things so often do. But then I got to know an independent, vulnerable, slightly bizarre girl who I enjoy sharing my time with. Sometimes you can't explain attraction. It's gravity. You know it's there, and it just, it just is.' He pushed a plate in my direction and we sat at the breakfast bar quietly eating while I contemplated just how right he was.

After dinner Anton suggested a walk on the beach. We came to rest a short distance from the sea. Everything burned gold as the sun began to set. Even in the evening haze it was possible to see across the water to Albania. It was so peaceful, with only one or two people much further along the beach. I dug my toes into the soft sand to delight in its cool, moist underbelly as

135

the waves unfolded in front of us. I was sat in front of Anton, snuggled into his cocoon. We were watching the sea leave marks in the sand as it melted through the grains. My back pressed against his chest as though he were my own personal armchair and his arms were a hairy blanket.

'When's your flight home?' His voice was low and warm on the tip of my ear.

'I don't know. Maybe ten or twelve days. I've lost track of it all. Why? Are you trying to get rid of me?'

'No, I don't want you to leave.' He pressed his chin gently on top of my head.

I inhaled the sea air deep into my lungs and tried to exhale the thought of leaving. However I looked at it, I would need to leave eventually. Anton brushed my hair to one side and kissed my neck. His left hand started to trace my body, across my arms and my legs, a touch as light as the breeze on my cheek. I pressed my back harder against his broad chest, solid and strong. The hand crept up my top and settled itself, causing a low, satisfied noise to vibrate from his chest.

'Naughty,' I said, and closed my eyes to absorb his touch. It all felt completely natural but with the thrill of new beginnings. I felt as though my blood pressure had increased in anticipation. As though every blood vessel in my body contained double its normal volume. I could feel every blood cell racing along carrying a backpack full of hormones and lust. His right hand swept across my abdomen, caressing, teasing then finding a button to undo... two, three and it disappeared.

'What are you doing...?' My words trailed off and dissolved into the sand with the sea.

He didn't answer, and I didn't protest. I didn't even think to glance around the beach. I was in a new moment; one I hadn't seen coming but relished nonetheless. My mind was blank and then suddenly full of colour as my head fell back onto his shoulder arching at his rhythm. I had to bite my own thumb to stop myself from crying out. He held me as I relaxed still inhaling deeply. Then I could feel his torso bounce under mine. He was laughing! Suddenly self-conscious, I whipped my head to look over my shoulder and confront him.

'What are you laughing about?' My skin was already washed with a rose tint, but it flushed deeper, even though I didn't know why he was giggling.

'You said it had been a while, but that was much too easy.' He bit his lips together in a playful line.

'Shut up, you arse!'

All this did was make him laugh harder, almost throwing me off his bouncing chest.

'I'm sorry, I'm sorry. I'm just happy. It's been a long time for me too you know.' There was a jovial suggestion in his tone.

'Well if you keep that up it'll be a lot longer too.'

He fell backwards into the sand with a smug little laugh joggling me back too. I arranged myself and staggered to my feet then turned around to face him with my fists pressed into my hips. 'Right, I think you should go home now. What are you doing tomorrow?'

I offered my hand to help him up but he grabbed my forearm and pulled me on top of him pressing me firmly to his body.

'Seeing you? Wait, I do have some work lined up tomorrow. Just driving some stuff back and forth.'

'Where?'

'Agios Stefanos again.'

'Can I have a lift, please? I might just hang out at some of the old haunts.'

'Get to mine at nine. I'm taking Gaia too.'

After he left I decided to stay on the beach. Clouds gathered into a leathery navy and grey swathe over the sea. As they rolled across, the breeze was firmer in its touch, with added lashes of sand. Another storm was growing about me, only this time it was different. I didn't feel alone any more; I was part of a family again. As lightning flashed over the sea, I smiled. I did miss Anton's presence, his incessant giggling, our little conversations – all of him. He gave me confidence to turn my back on the storm, unafraid of its strength. I strolled back to the house in a light rain with him lingering in my thoughts, filling them, taking them over. I packed a bag for the next day, just in case I could stay with him again. I sent him a simple message:

Dream well x

Chapter 17

Anton dropped Gaia and me off on the corner next to Silver Star where only days before we had been drinking milkshakes together.

'Are you in a rush to be anywhere?' I asked her, hopeful to have my milkshake partner again.

'Not particularly.'

'Would you like a milkshake?'

'I don't think I would be comfortable saying no.' She shrugged and flashed a cheeky grin as we crossed the road.

We gave a wave to the owner before Gaia sat at the same table as before. I hoped it would bring better luck this time.

'So, what's on your agenda today?' I asked.

'I'm going to Natalia's, before we help in the taverna again, washing up.' She exhaled and leant her face on her hand, swishing her mouth to one side with a cartoon-like pout.

'Well, at least it's money!'

'True. What are you doing? Dad said something about a frame?'

'I need to look for a photo frame for my mother. Your dad

139

has kindly printed out a photo for me so now I need a frame,' I told her.

'I'm glad you're trying again with your mum. What's the worst that could happen? If you don't like her at least you can say you tried,' she shrugged, as though my feelings were easy to set aside.

'*Kalimera*.' A loud voice was being aimed in our direction.

'Nico!' We spoke in unison, only I was rolling my eyes and Gaia's were wide and attentive. Our heads snapped round to look at each other, mouths open. We mirrored each other in surprise.

'*Boró na kathíso?*' he said.

Gaia quickly turned her attention back to him, nodded frantically and translated that he had asked to sit down. She wasn't looking at me though and her eyelashes were working overtime.

He pulled out a chair and sat back in it, placing one long foot onto the opposite knee. I was surprised he was able to sit in such a way — his black chino shorts were so tight on his slim thighs.

He said, 'How are the most beautiful girls in Agios Stefanos?'

He was very close to Gaia, who, to my horror, was swooning. Unfortunately, or perhaps fortunately for her, the attention felt like a game aimed at me. He was watching me as he put his arm over the back of her wicker chair.

'We're good, Nico.' she said, 'How do you know Melodie?' She knew we knew each other; she must, as she'd seen us talking to Ant only days ago. She'd turned herself into a mannequin as she positioned herself on the tip of her chair, crossing her legs and lightly placing her hands on her knee, head tilted on the side, waiting for his response.

'Melo? We go far back, don't we, Melo?'

'Yes, all of a week. He is a friend of a friend,' I snapped.

'Oh.' The poor girl looked bewildered and was blushing at having him so close to her. She started fiddling with the menu, eyes scanning across the road.

I was also turning red but for a different reason. 'Can we help you with anything, Nico?' I was flaring my nostrils and pressing my lips tightly together. Unlike Gaia, my hands were pressed firmly into the table. It wasn't going to help the situation; he took pleasure in winding me up.

'I saw you and I want to become the luckiest man in Corfu. So... I sit here.'

'Mmm.' I almost growled my little hum.

Gaia, on the other hand, started to look a little bit like she was watching a tennis match. Her eyes went back and forth, wide and curious.

I said, 'How do you two know each other?' I tilted my head and sipped my milkshake, waiting to hear an answer I approved of.

'Everyone knows Nico!' Gaia was grinning at him, long lashes still on form. Most of which was going unnoticed by Nico.

'Everyone knows Nico!' he repeated with a grin, then drew his thin fingers through his thick hair. 'I must leave. I'm sorry. *Tha milisouma argotera*.' With that he was up and walking away.

I jumped up to follow him, and tapped him frantically on his shoulder.

'Melo, I did not know you were that desperate. Well, I did.'

Electricity jolted through my right arm to my fingertips. I carefully pressed each fingernail into my thumbs, one by one, to keep my hands busy.

141

'You know she is thirteen! Ten years younger than you!' I said in my most aggressive, hushed tone.

'Really? Well, I thought she is sixteen at least. I'll have to wait a couple of years, no?' He laughed and turned to walk away.

'This is no joke,' I almost shouted. 'I don't want to see you leading her on again. Or you'll have me to answer to!'

'What are you? Her mother? I'm having fun. She's a kid. It's not her I have any interest in. Is it?' He pulled my hand from my side and kissed it.

This time when he walked away, I let him go. When I sat back at the table, Gaia was almost purple with questions and words.

'Seriously, how do you know Nico? He is so gorgeous!'

'Really?' I suppose his boyish looks and arrogance were a perfect storm for the hormones of any thirteen-year-old girl.

'Yes!'

'He is ten years older than you, so maybe focus on Finn instead.' Anton would hit the roof if he found out, I was pretty sure. I started aggressively scratching a bite on my ankle with my other foot.

'You sound worse than my dad!' Her top lip curled up.

'Sorry if I was a bit touchy about Nico. He can be a sarcastic little shit and he rubs me up the wrong way. That's not your fault. He is a handsome enough man...'

She snorted when I said "shit" forgetting her age; luckily I did a passable job of side-stepping it.

Her phone buzzed.

'Sorry, Melo, I should go,' she snorted again. 'I told Natalia I'd be late but she keeps texting.'

'That's fine, it was nice to hang out. Just – please don't call me 'Melo' again.'

She gave a laugh as she swung her bag up from under the table and onto her back.

'I won't. Thank you for the drink. I'm glad you can finish this time! See you later!'

I tapped my straw into the bottom of my half-empty glass. In all of Nico's nonsense, there was something that had really caught in my mind. He'd said, 'What are you? Her mother?' It hadn't occurred to me at the time that I was being over-protective. Anton could protect her in many ways, but she needed female guidance and it had meant a lot that she had spoken to me. She meant a lot to me, which was ridiculous.

I decided to have another milkshake and watch the world go by before bothering to move. It was quite empty until a family of four came in and sat a few yellow tables down from mine. There was a boy of perhaps only two or three, and a baby daughter. They'd been dressed in matching navy-and-white stripes. They were some of the most adorable children I'd ever seen — pretty little pixie faces with big eyes, and glowing with holiday excitement. I watched them from behind my sunglasses. The little boy kept trying to make his sister jump by shouting 'Boo!'. It didn't matter if he succeeded or not, he would let out a high-pitched squeal of a laugh. His baby sister would go from surprised to gurgling and giggling, jumping and wriggling in her mother's arms. Each time the blonde woman, their mother, would attempt to shush the little boy, to try to curb his excitement, to no avail. The long- haired man – clearly their father, based on looks alone – chatted to the owner about different ice cream flavours. I wanted that. Whatever it was that they had. That everyday stuff of being a family and bringing up children – the good, the bad, the

143

crazy. Even spending time with Gaia, who was far from a baby, gave me a sense of purpose. She made me want to become worthy of being looked up to, instead of the lonesome hermit I'd become.

'Nanny, Grandad! Look, I'm getting this one! Look!' The little boy suddenly squeaked with joy. My throat closed tightly around my tongue as the pair approached the table and sat down. My mama and papa would never know any children I may have, but, perhaps my mother and even my father might. With that, I knew I had to leave before tears appeared from under my glasses.

I meandered back to the supermarket, where I had previously bumped into Gaia, to look for a photo frame. They had a selection but most were indeed very touristy, with '"Corfu"' or '"San Stefanos"' written on them. This wasn't the right style for someone living on the island. Plus '"San Stef"' wasn't the proper name of the resort but one made up by a tour company so it wouldn't get confused with another Agios Stefanos on the island. Definitely not an appropriate gift for my mother. It suddenly struck me: there was a little shop, Taste Of Life, only a short march along the road; so off I went. I didn't know why I hadn't thought of it sooner. As soon as I stepped inside, I was surrounded by hand-crafted, unique little knick- knacks, and some not so little ones. It had the smell of freshly carved wood and olive soap. It was the kind of place that was so full, you would have to be careful that nothing attached itself to you without your knowledge. A breeze came in through the door behind me, setting off lots of the wind chimes around the shop in a plethora of wood and metal harmonies.

I took my time eyeing all of the treasures. I came across some frames and looked eagerly through them, settling on one with shells. It wasn't as though it would have anything to clash with in her living room, and it was rather sweet. I kept walking around — most of the gifts were locally sourced and handmade, from driftwood signs to olive wood sculptures. I found myself gently touching the curve of a wooden salad spoon, wondering if it was the type of thing my mother would like or needed, when I saw it. There, on a higher shelf, in amongst a whole wall of olive wood delights, was the most beautiful, hand-crafted photo frame. I put down the one in my hand and reached for it. Perfectly smooth to the touch, with naturally dark lines running through it. Two of the corners had been brought to points and the other two curved. The imperfectly perfect lines made it feel beautiful yet awkward. Just like my mother. I knew it was the right one. I pressed it against my chest. I had been worrying about finding the right sort of thing, and now I could relax that I'd made the right decision. It just felt right.

My second decision was to lie on the beach for the rest of the morning, hiring a sun lounger and snoozing. Other than being woken up by the resident fruit-seller, shouting about selling his grapes – or "gripes" – it was a peaceful time, one filled with a salty breeze that whipped me into a dream of Mama and Papa snoozing on the loungers next to mine. In that moment I believed they were there with me. I could hear Papa whisper 'Gripes' at me in response to the fruit-man. Then Mama tutted, saying, 'Oh Pete,' and I could smell her peony perfume twist in the air, dancing with the salt. My dozing left me feeling hollow; one moment they were close enough to touch, then I awoke without them.

I took a walk along the beach to Waves for lunch. I settled myself on the edge of their terrace looking out across the sand

145

and the sea. A perfect position for occupying the mind with people-watching. I had a craving for something comforting and they made a delicious deep-fried cheese ball thing. I can never remember the name of it but it was perfectly stringy, salty and yummy. A favourite of mine and Papa's. I decided to text Anton:

When you're done, come and be a tourist with me. I'm on the beach near Mango Bar – bring swim shorts (for a change)! x

I was waiting on the beach, catching up on Instagram behind my sunglasses, when I heard a familiar tone:

'Hello, tourist.'

'Well, hello. I'm so glad you're not the fruit-man again,' I said, rolling my eyes beneath my sunglasses as Anton sat on the lounger next to mine. 'You're in luck, I paid for that sun-bed too.'

'I have a small, or large, problem, depending on how you look at it.'

'Okay…' I sat up to face him, lifting my sunglasses onto my head.

'Unsurprisingly I don't keep swimwear in my van. I went to some of the supermarkets to see if I could find anything. The only thing near my size was still small for me.' He pulled out some tiny hot pants, sending me into a frenzy of belly laughs.

'Oh my,' I could barely breathe. 'You have to go and put them on! Go! Go!'

With some protest he got up like a sulky teenager who had been told to clean their room. He came out again in his normal clothes.

146

'Aww, where are they?' I pulled an over-exaggerated sad face. 'I'm in a bikini – it's no worse.' I waved my hand across my blue bikini top.

'They're underneath,' he said, looking down.

'Come on, then. Let's go for a swim!' I jumped up, eager to see his new purchase. The smile on my face was likely manic while I tried to suppress more giddy laughter. Anton shrugged off his clothes until he was down to his see-it-all pale green swim shorts. I was biting back my laughter.

'Well, at least you've got a lot to be proud of,' I said with a shrug, then threw my glasses on my sun lounger. Walking towards him, I slipped my hands under his arms and wrapped myself around him, our bodies sticking together in the heat.

'You smell like sun lotion.' He sniffed my shoulder, then gave it a little kiss.

'Come on,' I whined, 'let's swim.' Grabbing his wrist, I dragged his beautiful, tightly squeezed body down the beach and into the clear water. Once hidden under the waves he relaxed, with only the odd comment of discomfort. We swam, splashed and had fun. It was nice to do the tourist bit.

'Do you bother going on summer holidays when you live somewhere as beautiful as this?' I asked.

'I know a lot of people can't. They're too reliant on summer tourism to travel themselves. We don't often go on holiday. People visit us or we go to England. I like Gaia to spend time with her cousins there. We do like to go on an adventure, though. We have been to Thailand, Norway and a few other places.'

'Wow.' I paused, pondering my next question, lying back into the sea. 'So, do you think you'd ever move back there? to England, I mean.'

'No.'

'That was pretty down the line.'

'We wouldn't be able to have the lifestyle in England. It just wouldn't be possible. Our money goes further here. This is Gaia's home.' He gently patted the water with his hands. 'I do want her to go to university in the UK. That's years away, though.' Everything he said was logical. I had no argument to put forward. I stayed floating, drifting like a mildly deflated rubber ring that no one wanted to play with any more. I closed my eyes for a while as Anton held my hand and floated along next to me, his hair lightly tousled by the waves.

On the journey back to Anton's home, my brain was churning.

'You're quiet?' He said.

'Huh? Yeah. Sorry. I'm in my head.'

'Is it all too fast?'

'Probably.'

Then we fell silent again, sitting tentatively in the palm of fear, wondering what the future should be. I got into my car at his and went back to the Airbnb alone. It wasn't what I really wanted, but I thought it was perhaps what I needed. At least I was looking forward to talking to my mother about it all. Maybe she could help clear my mind the way Mama used to. Perhaps she had some helpful insight or experience of love and men that could help me work out what I was going to do.

Chapter 18

Liliana, my mother, my beautiful mother, had left the front door open to welcome me in.

'Hello?' I called in at the door.

'Come in!' She came down the narrow stairs, one foot meeting the other before taking the next. The opposite of Anton and Gaia.

'I left the door open for you. I've made lamb kleftiko. I hope that's okay?'

Leaving the door open hadn't done much in the way of cooling the room down.

I said 'Sounds and smells wonderful!'

'It won't be ready for a little while. Would you like a drink?'

'Just water, please.' I sat down in the hard red armchair, and as I did so, an old smell of smoke lifted from the fibres, adding to the thick air. It made me want to choke and open up a line of questions I didn't know if I could ask. She set my water on the nest of tables with a smile. We were still very awkward together. I wanted to break down the barriers of the past, but being around her made my hands and feet sweat.

'I was hoping you could help me. I need boy advice. I always used to talk to Grandmama about things and thought maybe you could help.'

'Okay. I can't say I have much experience, to be honest. I could help with cooking. Or gardening.' As she spoke, I thought how she reminded me of a fine little squirrel. She spoke quietly and quickly, sudden moves seemed to frighten her, and she had some quirky movements too.

'Oh, come on. That can't be true,' I laughed. 'You had me at sixteen! Plus, you're a beautiful woman.'

She shifted uncomfortably and the smile went from her face.

'I really haven't. I don't think I'd be very helpful.'

My disappointment turned towards hurt. I picked up my glass, taking a sip of water to calm and focus myself. I sat looking down at the liquid – clear, see-through. No promise of anything but clarity. I wished Liliana could have said the same.

'Oh, well, as you haven't opened up about things, I didn't realise. It just seems odd to claim to have no experience and yet you've had a child.'

Her face pulled into flat lines – her brows, her mouth. Even her nose flattened to her face. The look was so very similar to Grandpapa. Funny how much she looked like Mama, but her expressions were Grandpapa. She didn't want to have the conversation. She was ready to shut down again.

I said, 'I know I agreed to leave the past in the past and just get to know the now, but that seems pretty hard. Of course I have so many questions – who wouldn't? I'd like advice about Anton from Grandmama, but I'm stuck with you, and even asking you for that means talking about some of your life for the past thirty-one years. I mean, what have you been up to in that time? Why did you never visit me? why — ' I caught myself, paused, and took a breath. 'Sorry. I'd like us to actually form a real bond, if that's even possible.'

'I understand. As I said before, I've been here for fourteen years...'

I wanted to shake her slender shoulders until she told me something. I wanted to rummage around the house for evidence of the life she had chosen over me, and find out if it was worth it. I needed something, anything, tangible.

'And what about before that? Have you had boyfriends? Do I have siblings? Have you always lived alone? You've told me nothing real.'

'It too difficult to explain,' she whispered. 'I'll try to help you with the Anton problem. I'll try. Tell me.'

My emotions were rattling around in my chest and it hurt to hold it all in. I wanted her in my life, a link to my true parents, the only ones who were there for me.

'Okay,' I began then had to stop and fight my urge to cry. I just wanted my grandparents back. All the willpower, all the desire in the world couldn't change it. I couldn't wish for it and they would be there; they weren't going to magically appear. I was stuck with her and she wouldn't even have a proper conversation with me. I swallowed it all back and started again. 'Well, I really like Anton. I feel like it could go somewhere, and I had hoped to have a relationship with you too, but I live in Cambridgeshire. Between finding him and then you, I've been considering moving here or at least extending my trip. I don't know. I just want help.'

'Please don't change your plans on my account. Don't bring me in as a factor.'

Beads of sweat were accumulating under my heavy, loose

hair, making me itch. I scratched at the back of my neck, hard, and squirmed a little, not knowing what to say.

'Okay, well that puts me in my place. You won't share your life with me, you don't want to be factored into my future...' My innards were stripped raw and strung out on a line. I closed my eyes for a moment. Just a split second, to step into the darkness of my lids. When I was a child, I liked to hide in my cupboard to let the darkness hold me. I would sometimes sit and consider what was wrong with me, why my mother didn't want me. Darkness became a blanket to hide in and I wanted more than anything to be back in that cupboard with my thoughts instead of my reality.

'No, that's not what I meant.'

Her words didn't matter. I

stood up, ready to leave.

'I was abducted!' she shouted, eyes looking at the floor by my feet.

I just stood there; the only movement was her index finger tapping at her leg.

'Abducted? What do you mean? What are you talking about?' I was trying to stay strong but there was a distinct quiver to my voice. I fell back down into the chair, hurting my tailbone and surrounding myself in smoky air again.

'I really don't want to talk about it. I just – I don't want you to leave, and I need you to know I wouldn't leave you. I didn't leave you. I was taken away from you.' She still didn't look at me.

'You can't say something like that and not explain more.

I'm your daughter. You can tell me – I want to be here for you.' My mouth was saying the right things and sounding calm too, but my brain was skipping from one reality to the next.

She started shaking her head, so I continued talking. 'I'm so confused. Grandmama and Grandpapa would have looked for you if you'd been abducted. It's surely impossible.' My heart was pounding harder as I considered the idea that she might be the victim in all of this, and not me.

'It's not impossible. It's what happened.' She looked up, frowning at me. 'I never thought I'd see you again, ever.' Her voice was hushed, but, to me, it cut through the dense air like a samurai sword.

'How do you explain your letter, then? Saying you didn't want a baby and you weren't coming back?' I said, as my fingers dug into the wooden arms of the chair.

'What?' Her eyes turned into pale blue slits.

'The letter. The police even said because of the letter there was little they would do. You said not to bother looking for you, you were already gone.' My voice mimicked her whispered tones; the room was so void of soft furnishings it almost echoed.

'I didn't write a letter. I didn't.'

'It was typed, but you had signed it. The signature matched your handwriting.'

'No, I didn't. I didn't write a letter.'

'I've seen the letter and I've seen your writing on cards and school-work. It matched. You left me in my pram and that letter on the door-mat.'

'No, you're wrong.' Her voice may have been soft, but there was stone behind it now. She meant it and I believed her.

'Okay, how then? Why? Who?' I was stuttering questions in confusion.

Looking at me, she lifted the corners of her mouth in a bewildering smile.

153

'I remember that day. The last day I got to hold you, feed you, touch your soft skin.' She sniffed. 'I need to check on the dinner – it'll be ready soon!' And then she was gone.

I was suddenly alone in her living room, with a cold sweat penetrating the heat. Should I get up and follow? Should I push the point? As my eyes darted around the blank room, I remembered the photo frame in the car. I got up to get it but opening the front door was no quiet job. I had to lift and tug with a clunk on its hinges. My mother came flying out of the kitchen with a wooden spoon in the air.

'Please don't leave! Please! It was your father – your father abducted me! Please just stay for dinner at least. I don't want to lose you again – I can't!'

I became numb, other than the strangest sensation, almost like the tingle of pins and needles, filling my fingers and toes. My breath became jagged and I just stood holding the door open, mouth open, car key in hand. Eventually I managed to croak out something about going to the car to get something.

'Oh.' She lowered her spoon. I don't think she intended to harm me with it but she'd had a crazed look about her when she flew into the room, with eyes red from fighting back tears and her washed-out wavy hair fluffy with static like it'd been rubbed with a balloon. 'I'm just dishing up.' She said. Don't be long.' With a slight rib twitch, she turned back to the kitchen.

I didn't know what to say in response to her outburst so I just carried on to the car. When I came back, the fold-up dining table was out and she was placing the two armchairs beside it. I think my mouth had stayed open the whole time.

Chapter 19

'I thought we would eat indoors it's more civilised,' she said.

I didn't reply; I just sat down, still holding the gift all wrapped in tissue paper. She was starting to lay the table around me: knives, forks, salt, pepper, rattan place mats, then food. Not a word was spoken. Only when she sat down did I pass the gift across the table. The first gift from my hands to hers. She took it carefully and unwrapped it slowly. Her whole face lifted into a smile as she saw the photo of us. She gently stroked the glass with her thumb then pressed it to her chest, just as I had. A tear tripped and danced its way down her face.

'I'm sorry to blurt that out. I didn't want you to find out like that. I didn't want you to find out at all.' She placed the photo on the table, wiped her cheek and indicated to me to start eating.

My stomach was pulling, churning, and acid burned at my throat. It didn't matter; I picked up my cutlery and proceeded as instructed. The delicate lamb fell apart and filled the room with the smell of oregano and onions. I managed two mouthfuls before my cutlery was down.

'I need to know more. I'm sorry but I do. My father abducted you? Why? What happened? Does that mean he wrote the letter? How? Everyone thought you'd run away. The letter made sense to everyone...'

'So truly no one ever looked for me? I guess it's no surprise. I wasn't easy to live with as a teen. I would never have left you, though. Not out of choice. No matter what he wrote in some stupid letter.' She didn't look up from her plate. 'I loved you. He had to drag me away from you kicking and screaming. Now please eat your dinner. Unless you don't like it. I can make something else. I have some pasta.' She was already starting to stand up.

'No, no! This is delicious!' By way of proof, I began to eat with vigour, hoping it could earn me more information.

Kicking and screaming? Abducted by my father? Nothing was making any sense to me, and the last thing I wanted to do in that moment was eat a lamb dinner and be civilised. The heat and the information curdled in my belly. It made it hard to keep eating, but I did, quickly. She was watching me out of the corner of her eye, until she had enough of my haste. She dropped her knife and fork in a clatter. There was a long silence; she choked on her food a little and scrambled for her napkin to cover her mouth.

'The man who had got me pregnant, your father, took me from my home. I didn't want to leave you. I didn't want to be with him. He took me. Eventually, he brought me here and I lived as his wife until he died seven years ago. I lived in fear for most of my life.' She spluttered a little, but her words were firm but calm. She didn't look at me; instead she carefully picked up her knife and fork to eat. As though that was it. I could tell she wouldn't say more. I decided to bide my time.

'Do you like the frame?' I managed to rouse a smile from her round lips. She had made more effort that day. At some point before dinner, she had pulled her hair back into a bun and was wearing a little lip balm, or maybe gloss, across her lips. Her terracotta dress was the worse for wear but was an improvement on the T-shirt and old trousers of our first two encounters.

'I love it, thank you. It's so very kind of you. At last I have something worth displaying.' Thirty-one years and nothing to display. What sort of life had it been?

'I'm pleased you like it.' Three more mouthfuls and I'd be done.

'I do. It's so beautifully carved. I'm not sure if I'll keep it down here or put it upstairs.'

Two more mouthfuls and I'd be done.

'I think down here, perhaps. I probably spend more time down here.'

One more mouthful. Done.

'You know,' She said. 'I still can't believe you're here. You're beautiful.'

'Thank you.' Instinctively I looked down at my dress and brushed my hands across the soft fabric. It was the same purple one I had worn on my birthday. I'd wanted to make an effort for our first family meal. She looked at me with sombre eyes. She was slow to finish eating, chewing each mouthful carefully. As soon as she was done, I had to start again.

'Grandmama and Grandpapa said you left. They really thought you'd run away, left me. You said "kicking and screaming"? Surely you knew about the letter? I'm so confused!'

'You're confused? I hadn't. I wouldn't. All I can think is

157

he did it straight after taking me.' She stood up, picked up the plates and was back off to the kitchen, leaving me once again. This time I started putting everything back where it came from, like a child tidying toys at night, desperate for story time. Only this felt more like watching a horror story unfold.

Sh returned and we sat for a moment. I knew I'd have to start, have to nudge her to talk. There was no way it would come out naturally.

'So...Why did he abduct you?' In my mind they were in love. He was too passionate and she was using him as a cover. A cover for wanting to leave me. She was only young and an unplanned pregnancy was a lot less romantic than coming to live in Corfu.

Her hands pressed her head, and she took a few deep breaths before she began, hands falling over her eyes for an extra moment as she began to open up.

'Because he was evil. When I was fifteen, he was twenty-eight. Back then I thought he loved me.' Her hands rubbed her temples before they dropped to her lap.' He would treat me, take me to expensive restaurants and such. Back then he was quite good-looking too, and I used to lie and tell Mum and Dad I was going out with my friends. I knew they wouldn't let me spend time with someone so much older. They would've been right, of course.' She spoke softly and steadily, not looking at me. I was spinning again with the new information. Fifteen and twenty- eight? 'For a short time, he locked me in a room in his house, not far from Mum and Dad. He told me you'd be better off without me and, with time, I believed him. Even now, looking at you, I can't help but think he was right. He told me no one wanted me and no one was looking for me. I guess he was right on both counts.' She looked at her hands ruefully, and clenched them like screwed-up paper, before releasing them and looking at me.

'You're here now,' she said. Her round eyes became wide as she looked me over. I thought I likely looked rather ill; I felt ill. Fifteen and twenty-eight. With so many thoughts in my head everything was starting to turn into confetti, thrown in the air and impossible to retrieve.

'So, wait' —I managed to catch a thought— 'who was he? My father?' My father the child abductor, a confetti piece I wish I hadn't caught.

'His name was Adam Jones. He worked in banking – he was very intelligent, always good with numbers and statistics.'

This was bizarre.

'Wait —' I caught some more confetti. 'You said he died seven years ago – that's plenty of time to find me. Grandmama and Grandpapa lived in the same house you grew up in, so I wasn't exactly hard to find!' I was thinking more clearly and snapped a little. My emotions were running high and her house was as hot as a cauldron.

Her eyes snapped into focus.

'After over twenty years of emotional and physical abuse, I didn't believe any of you would be interested in seeing me. You didn't look for me – he told me you weren't. He obviously knew about the letter, and I didn't. At first, I used to try to check newspapers, but there was never a sign that they had looked for me. And – and – I couldn't go...'

'Why? Why not?'

'No, I – I just – I knew that Mum and Dad would keep you safe, and I just held onto that. I always thought of you, every day – what you were doing, what you looked like, if you liked drawing or dolls, sports or science. But I was afraid, I was a fool.'

I felt like I was outside my body. The only thing that kept me knowing I was still inside it was the urge to vomit. I had to excuse myself to her bathroom. Within moments I was upstairs in her home clinging to a pale peach, pristine sink, looking into a cabinet mirror. Looking down at my purple dress, I felt a little silly, embarrassed at my own sexuality. I shook my head, making hair stick to my face. There was just me, my shallow breathing and the reflection. It's not about you, I told myself, it's about her, your mother, who didn't leave you, who was taken from you. I ran cold water on my hands and combed it through my hair with my fingers, taking comfort in the familiar sensation. Stepping out of the bathroom, I could see into her bedroom which, again, was a hollow space that comfort had forgotten. One bed, one cupboard, two cabinets – nothing more, not even an extra pillow. I took my time creaking down the stairs to meet my mother, who sat patiently waiting for my return.

'This is a lot to take in,' I said. 'When I first met you, I just thought you were embarrassed about leaving me, or you just didn't want me around. I never imagine—'

'I didn't want you to know what your father was like. I wanted to keep protecting you from him.'

'Keep protecting? What do you mean, *keep*?'

'Hmph…' She rubbed her forehead with aggressive fingers. She wriggled in her chair, pulling at the hem of her dress to tug it over her knees before continuing. 'He said if I left him, he would hurt you, so I never left him. I never tried to run. I would rather he hurt me than you, and I couldn't risk it now, could I? It's not as though you would have been hard to find. You said that yourself.'

My incredible, strong mother.

'So you spent your whole life saving mine and I didn't even know? I wish you had come back.' The air felt so heavy and my chest was so tight it was like taking in water; drowning in the information, and I couldn't swim. But still, I had to know more. 'What actually happened back then? Start from the beginning, I'm getting so confused.'

'Well, as I said, we started going out when I was fifteen. We actually met at a friend's party; he, Adam, would treat me so well. He made me happy at first, always the gentleman, opening doors for me and telling me how pretty I was – flowers, chocolates, anything I wanted. Then, when I turned sixteen, he started to force himself on me, saying I owed him. It was very confusing because he had been so loving and charming, and some days he still was, then the next day he would be forceful and aggressive and violent. Sometimes he would tell me I made things up and I would wonder if it was all a bad dream. It was only looking at my bruises that kept my sanity at times. When I found out I was pregnant with you I was too afraid to tell anyone. I only admitted it to myself when I was over six months gone; I told Mum but there was no way I could say who the father was – I didn't dare – and it caused so many arguments. I wish I had said now. I was a child myself when I look back – I was stupid and naive. My parents wouldn't let me out after I told them I was pregnant. I hadn't seen him in months. It was difficult at sixteen with teenage hormones and pregnancy hormones too; I used to kick back a lot and there was only my parents to take it all out on. I didn't want a baby – I'm sorry, but I didn't. It was only once you arrived that it changed. The day he came and took me I think he was shocked to find me with a baby. He

161

was so angry. I don't know if he had planned to take me – I never asked – not that he would have told me if I had. I had been about to take you out for a walk – your first outing in the pram Mum and Dad had got you. He pushed the pram back inside the door, slammed it shut and took me. Well, that's the simple, less violent version.'

The silence. Silence to absorb my father's name: Adam. Silence to absorb what he was: violent. Silence to hold in my urge to cry.

'Can I have some more water, please?'

She jumped up and scurried off into the kitchen. My mouth was dry from holding it slightly open. I couldn't breathe. It was like the tiny room was getting smaller and yet the contents were somehow getting bigger. I tried to inhale and I couldn't; my throat was closing up. I groped at my neck and broke the necklace I was wearing. I didn't care. I had to leave. The door had been left ajar and I ran out of it, still clutching the necklace. The blood-red sunset blinded me and the wind slapped my face. I managed a small breath. I was hunched over, holding my knees and shaking, ready to fall. Liliana, my mother, my beautiful mother, was by my side holding my arm. She knelt, bare knees in the dirt, to see my face and to stroke my hair. She reminded me so much of Mama; she would have been a wonderful mum if she hadn't been taken from me. I felt so bad at how angry I had been at her for so many years; I still felt anger that she could have found me seven years ago, but I tried to see how she must have felt. Everything was spinning. I could hear her voice, soothing and calm in my ear, but I don't remember the words. I just remember her eyes stayed on me as she led me back into the house.

She got a fan and plugged it in right next to me.

'Is that better? Sorry it gets so hot in here – I can't afford air conditioning. I guess I'm mostly used to it now, after so many years.' She was back to kneeling by my side and clutching the arm of the chair.

'I'm sorry.' My voice was quiet against the power of the fan. 'I couldn't breathe, I needed air.'

She got up and grabbed the glass of water from the little table.

'Here. Drink your water.' I took it and sipped slowly. It did help. It gave me something new to focus on. The fan was blowing my hair fiercely, making my ears ring.

'All these years I thought you didn't want me. If we'd known... You realise we were all coming to this island for holidays? Most years. I mean, other Greek islands too, but... you were less than an hour away from us.'

'I chose the island. He told me we had to go. We couldn't stay in England. We were in a few different countries following his work – Germany for six or seven years – all over the place really. Eventually, I persuaded him to come here. I would tell him stories of the Greek islands – this one in particular. I'm sure you know we used to holiday in Sidari. I hoped that one day I might be lucky enough to see my parents on holiday. Sometimes I could persuade him to take me to Sidari for the day – although not very often. In my head you were still a baby, of course, and I'd pick you up and never let go.'

'Can we sit outside? In the shade?' I couldn't bear the closed-in walls any longer.

She led me through the small galley kitchen and outside. There were white chairs and a round table underneath a greying umbrella. I stumbled towards them. Slumping over the table. The metal table dug into my arms.

'You were only, what, forty when he died? That's so young. You're so young *now*.'

Even though she'd had a hard life, she was full of potential. I wanted to dress her, do her hair and makeup.

'I feel about a hundred,' she laughed. 'I have for thirty-one years. I'm so happy you're here. Please don't hate me...' Her voice was pleading on the breeze and she carefully laid her hands on the table.

The more I looked at her, the more everything fell into place. Her odd little ticks, her – at times – stilted movements, all too well thought out. You can't brush twenty years of abuse under the table. She needed me as much as I needed her.

I told her I didn't hate her; how could I? She had just been a child. I wanted to reassure her. Only, the desire to run away and hide from the thought of my biological father kidnapping, raping and beating my mother was overwhelming. If I hadn't had more questions, perhaps I would have left then. I asked her if there had been others like me, the undesired result of rape. In a strange way, I was hopeful.

Her lip trembled when I asked, and her chest heaved and her fingers pinched at her knobbly brown knees.

'A son. Your brother, Phillip.'

I let out an elated gasp. I wanted to know everything about him. Where he was, how old he was. She was pointing to the back of the small rectangular garden. Her shoulders rounded and caved in, then her head dropped and shook. Without a word I walked to where she had pointed. There, pressed into the dry ground of Corfu, stood a small wooden cross with "P.J." scratched into it. I squatted down next to it. It was the sort of headstone you'd give a beloved family pet. I had to touch it to check if my eyes were seeing it correctly. The edges were sharp and sun- bleached. I could hear my heartbeat as my jugular throbbed.

'What on earth happened?'

'I could hide it for a long time, being pregnant. I thought I might be able to keep it. I must have been eight months when he realised. He didn't want children...' She paused and looked up to the sky. 'He was a sadistic man. He – he beat me but with purpose – he really didn't want children. It brought on early labour and I was in and out of consciousness. I remember him pacing and swearing at one point and, it was the strangest thing, I was there in the pain of it one moment then it was like a dream, like it wasn't real. When I eventually came round, I mean, really came round, the house was quiet. I begged to see the baby; they'd need feeding. He just shrugged, said, "It's dead." Eventually he told me it was a boy, and he'd named him Phillip and buried him without me. I'd been so sure I'd heard him cry – it must have been in my dream.' Her voice was barely audible; tears streamed from her eyes but she didn't bawl. She didn't scream or shout. Her eyes were bloodshot and set in pink rings from rubbing the lines of tears away. The tip of her nose had gone red too but that was it. I felt ashamed of myself. For everything. For not knowing sooner, for my own self-pity for years on end, for snapping at her and for not enjoying life when I had the freedom to do so.

I crouched down next to the little wooden cross and hid my face in my hands. My shoulders gave away my sob, juddering uncontrollably until I couldn't keep it in at all and I gasped for air before letting out everything I'd been holding back. I cried for her, for my lost brother, for myself, for the time we'd lost.

'I'm so sorry,' I wailed. 'I had no idea. All these years. I'm so sorry.'

She led me back to my chair and carefully stroked my hair as my head bent over my lap. I was swaying, knowing I should comfort her, not the other way around.

'Melodie, it's okay, my beauty,' she soothed. 'Do you know why I named you Melodie?' I shook my head and looked up at her through my hair. 'No, of course you don't; how could you? Well, you're my heart's song. As soon as I saw you, I loved you. I hadn't chosen you, or the situation, but my heart wanted to sing, so I sang to you – that was the first thing I did. I didn't say hello. Mum was there with me when I gave birth to you – the midwife passed you to my arms and I started to sing, and you stopped crying for a moment. So I called you Melodie. My beautiful baby. I was always just happy you never had to know him and you could live a happy, safe life. One I would love to know about. If you wouldn't mind telling me? To have you here, to see your face. It's more than a dream come true.' She started to choke on her words a little and cough.

'What was it? The song?'

'"You are My Sunshine".'

Mama had never told me that. She had been there and she never said. She had sung that to me whenever I was frightened or sad. I rubbed my face; my hands were covered in black from my mascara. I couldn't imagine what I looked like. My mother went and got me a box of tissues. I'd always desperately wanted to know why she had chosen the name Melodie. I never thought I'd know the answer.

'It's just so overwhelming to find out that your father is an evil bastard and your mother is an innocent victim' —I blew my nose— 'when you've spent your whole life imagining your father was a clueless teen and your mother was a selfish slut. I'm sorry – I didn't mean it like that!' I stuttered.

166

'Perhaps it would have been better if that's what you still thought. Instead of the truth of that horrible man. I'm glad my parents never knew the truth. I wouldn't want to have caused them more pain.'

'Don't be ridiculous.' I had to snap this time. 'They loved you, and nothing hurt more than not having you in their life, nothing.' I grabbed her hand to reassure her and for a split second I saw the flinch in her body language at suddenly being grabbed, then her relaxing when she looked at me.

I asked a lot of questions. Perhaps too many questions. I don't know why, but I had to know. Perhaps in an attempt to suffer as she had, in the knowledge of the truth. She told me of the abduction. How he grabbed her hair, kicked my pram and threatened to kill me if she didn't shut up. She was always more afraid of the possibility he would go back and hurt me than the things he would do to her. She stopped fighting back early on, as the beatings wouldn't last as long as she let him get on with it. She had been hospitalised on multiple occasions. Mostly bad cuts, like the silver line on her face; on close inspection there were many. But that wasn't all: broken ribs, wrist and fractured cheekbone. He died seemingly suddenly, finding out very late on that he was riddled with cancer; he had been the smoker in the house and it caught up with him. She didn't have much money as he never let her work or have access to money. Although he bought the house outright, he gambled most of his wages away. When he died she found accounts with a little bit of money in; she got a job in a supermarket, first as a cleaner, then on the checkout. She didn't have any friends and kept herself to herself. She didn't come back for me because she thought I'd be better off without her and she thought her parents didn't want her back – that they had never looked for her. I didn't understand why, not really, but then I hadn't lived through everything she had been through.

When I said goodbye to her, it wasn't particularly late but I was exhausted.

Holding my hands tightly, she said, 'Do what makes you happy while you can. That's my advice with Anton.'

I squeezed her tightly.

'Thank you,' I whispered in her ear, and kissed her cheek, soft with the scent of sweet almond. 'I like your necklace. It matches my ring,' I said. She pressed her fingers over the round opal and silver chain.

'Mum and Dad got it for my sixteenth birthday.' She displayed it between her bitten nails.

'Same,' I said and showed her my ring. We smiled for a moment, with nothing else that could be said. She had to work over the next few days so I agreed I would visit later in the week. As I drove away, I couldn't believe she was real, let alone who she was and what she had been through. My mind felt pitch black, back in the wardrobe I sat in as a child; it didn't feel like a comfort any more; now it was a vacuum, with a new type of grief.

Chapter 20

When I got back, I had a message from Ant – a little blue emoji heart. I wondered why blue. I didn't want to speak to anyone, so I sent the same back to him. I started to draw a bath, only to change my mind. I needed to wash off the horror of the day; a cold shower felt like a better option. My phone buzzed – Anton:

Please let me know you're back safe x

I stood in the shower. Still and cold. Eventually I made my hands wash my hair and I got out shaking. A stark contrast to the heat of my mother's home. I needed to distance myself from it all. From the knowledge of who had a hand in my creation.

Back safe. Speak tomorrow x

Yes, he did make me happy. Very happy. I needed to drink. I wanted my grandparents.

I found myself sitting in my car heading to Agios Stefanos. The place where I felt close to them and it would be acceptable to be drunk. My hair was still dripping on my shoulders when I arrived. I instinctively went to Vicky's. I marched straight to the bar.

'You're not Stavros!' I said as Nico turned round to face me. The bar was quiet – only two tables taken.

'Can't keep away from me.' His arrogant smile was really starting to get on my last nerve.

'Seriously, why are you working here?'

'I am happy to help in most bars when people need nights off.'

'I'll go somewhere else.' I tapped the bar and walked away. I couldn't be bothered with him. I wanted to wallow. Wallow in all of my loss – my grandparents, my brother and the thirty-one years I lost my mother because of that man.

'Wait! It's from me! Here – ouzo! You can't leave it – I've poured now.' He knew how to stop me in my tracks.

'Fine. Thank you.' I downed the drink, ice painfully hitting my teeth. I slammed down the glass.

'Another! It'd be rude not to drink. Or we could play I Have Never?' He laughed as he pushed the glass along the bar.

'Will all my drinks be free?'

'All from this.' He shook the half-empty bottle at me.

I wasn't going to turn down a fast drink. I drank again and he refilled. This time I took my glass and walked out of the bar, around the curve of the swimming pool and over to the corner of the paving to listen to the sea below. I stood leaning on the rail, focusing on the simple times I'd had. Eventually I was staring at the melted ice at the bottom of my glass. Three ouzos had warmed me, but it was time for another; I was looking for oblivion again. I could hear footsteps coming up next to me. I knew it was him – only he could have such a cocky stride.

'Good timing.' I held my glass out to Nico, who had brought the bottle to me. My face was pressed into my other hand, leaning on a pillar. Maybe I was swaying. His eyes wandered along my skin as he poured.

'What's wrong?' he asked, raising an eyebrow.

'Don't ask.' If I didn't want to talk to Anton, I certainly didn't want to talk to him. I drank my ouzo in one again so he could fill me up and, hopefully, leave me alone.

'It is too late. I ask already.'

'If you carry on, I'll go pay for my alcohol somewhere else.'

He laughed and left me alone. He left the bottle on a white plastic table that sat between two sun loungers. Perhaps I should've given him a little more credit. He was helping me get drunk, at least. The bar was empty. Maybe it was late? I had no idea.

He was cleaning glasses when I decided to leave and do the polite thing and say goodbye.

'Nice to see you again, Nico. Thanks for the booze.' I gave a strange, drunken salute and started to walk away. With one hop he was over the bar and catching up with me.

'Wait, wait! Come on, you must sit and have one drink with me.' He threw the tea towel across his shoulder and pouted under the shadow of his nose.

I shrugged; my resolve was very low.

I pulled out one of the heavy chairs, scraping and screeching it along the floor. In doing so we both recoiled and shivered. I sat down while he got the drinks. Everything was starting to sway with more vigour, or perhaps I was. He walked around with two beautiful, tall cocktail glasses. Both filled with orange liquid, straws, and plastic stirrers of flamingos and ladies.

'Sexy Greek?' I asked.

'Aww, thank you for noticing.' He had the potential to make my eyes hurt from my frequent rolling. 'I thought the juice might be good for you.'

'Thanks.' I held the glass tightly; it was my fragile anchor.

'You talk to me. I am a person.' His tone was soft, which was confusing more than anything. I did enjoy his Greek accent, though. I found it comforting.

'A sarcastic, arrogant person.' I snorted.

'Who gets you drinks. We could be a good matz.' He shrugged.

'"Matz"? Oh, you meant "match".' I smiled and circled my flamingo in my drink.

'Yes, that's what I said – matz.'

To be fair to him, he was being nice enough. I felt bad for being so rude, even through my drunken haze.

'I like your accent – it's the best part of you,' I laughed. 'Well, as you so desperately want to know what's in my head, it turns out my mother lives here on the island. I went to meet her. She was abducted by my father when I was a baby. She was only sixteen and my grandparents thought she had run away, so they didn't look too hard for her. Plus, they had me to deal with. My father, he used to beat her and rape her. She just had a horrible life, horrible, just horrible. I came here to get drunk to feel closer to my grandparents, who raised me. I'm just bloody lost, okay?'

'Fuck. Okay. Yes. Super difficult one,' he stuttered. 'I see why you want drink.' He took a cigarette out of its packet and passed me the rest. I didn't take one but I was depressed enough to be tempted.

172

'Yeah, well, now you know, huh? Lucky old you.'

'I always feel lucky to look at you, Melo.' He was trying to make my eyes hurt again.

'I'm going now. I'm drunk enough. I might be able to sleep now without my brain hurting from being overly loaded.'

'Overloaded,' he smirked, sitting up tall in his chair and dusting off his shoulder.

'That's what I said. And hey! I don't correct all the stuff you say wrong.'

'No, just some. I use three languages. You?'

I gave a pathetic shrug and slumped back in my chair.

'Hmm, it's my fault you're drunk. I'll get you home.' I nodded. I really was very drunk. 'Do you have a car? I drive a motorcycle.'

'Bloody typical,' I huffed. 'Yes I do. I have a hirer car.' He was laughing at me. 'What do you think you are laughing at? Mr? Huh?'

'You – you drunk.'

'It's you are drunk,' I said, stabbing my index finger towards him and squinting one eye.

'No. You are a drunk.'

Chapter 21

I woke up by rolling into a hard lump on my bed. The lump groaned at me, making every muscle in my body tense. I stayed still, waiting breathlessly to unravel what was going on.

'*Kalimera*,' groaned Nico.

'What the hell are you doing in my bed?' I still didn't make a move and my voice sounded like a hoarse robot.

'Aww, I'm sad you don't know.' He rolled over to face me with a big grin on his stupid baby face.

'Nico, what the bloody hell happened?' My voice was low and aggressive. I was ready to strike.

'Nothing, fool. You fell asleep in the car and you didn't wake, so I carried you up. I took off your stupid shoes. I only stay to keep an eye on you. I was worrying.'

'Oh. Thank you. Sorry, I just don't remember.'

It was his turn to roll his eyes at me, apparently. He got up and went to the bathroom.

I hid my face under the sheet. The only things I could remember after being in the bar were nightmares. A restless night with the things I had heard and the brother I had gained

174

and lost. I held my face tightly with both hands, wishing I could forget.

My phone was ringing. I eventually found it on the floor and answered, my head pounding from reaching towards the floor. It was Anton. His voice had a sing-song tone and he wanted to know when he would see me, how it all went, did I know anything new? I didn't want to say anything on the phone. I kept it short and neat – I would be there in an hour or two. By the time I hung up, my stomach felt like someone was whisking it with last night's ouzo. Nico walked back into the room in just his pants. It wasn't the same as looking at Anton, that was for sure. His lean muscular legs strutted confidently into the room, then he stood at my feet with his arms folded.

'I need a lift,' he said.

'Shit. Fine. Give me a minute.' I showered and got ready in record time just to make sure I could eat something, anything, before leaving the house. I had thrown on some clothes; black shorts, black crop top with a black crochet dress over. I looked like I was in mourning; I felt like it too. Luckily, my head was feeling a lot better by the time I eventually pulled up at Anton's. I stepped into a brief kiss, then I noticed Gaia hovering near the sofa.

'*Kali*, Melodie.' She gave a slightly awkward wave.

'Dad said you were seeing your mum yesterday. How's it going now?'

I had no desire to tell anyone the things in my head – what I had found. But without Gaia I wouldn't have known a thing. She deserved to know at least part of the story. I sat down and they both followed suit. I told them the very basics. No details. Looking at them as I spoke, I wondered if I had looked more or less stunned. They didn't interject all that much. Anton mostly scratched his stubbled chin and Gaia had tucked herself into the corner off the sofa, knees pulled tightly into her chest. I didn't hesitate; if I had, I would never have said a word. Halfway through Ant got up and sat beside me, taking one of my hands in both of his.

'What she has been through... I couldn't tell you it all — it's too horrific — but the one thing in it all is that she loved me. She didn't leave me.' I creased my eyes in an attempt to smile. Of course I was pleased she hadn't chosen to abandon me; only, the circumstances made me want to tear the world to shreds and set light to what was left.

Gaia started to talk then paused, still considering her words. 'If your father died, why didn't she find you?' True to form, her inquisitive nature came first. She untucked herself, stretching her long slim legs and placing her feet firmly on the ground.

'I asked the same thing. Lack of confidence, lack of funds. But mostly the first one. He told her that we wouldn't want her and would never forgive her.' Gaia was nodding and biting her lip. I don't think she really understood; in reality none of us could.

'She wasn't much older than you when she was taken – only a couple of years.'

'Wow, I'm so sorry for her – for you. I think I should leave you two. I'll go see if my friends are about.'

Gaia and Anton then continued the conversation in Greek. He got up and gave her some money. She ran upstairs, two by two, and came down with her backpack. 'I'm glad for you, that she didn't leave you, Melodie. Like my mum, it wasn't her choice.' And with that she left. I desperately wanted to change the subject and take the emotional limelight off me.

I said, 'What actually happened with Gaia's mother? You

said she was there when she died?'

Anton nodded towards the door.

'Mmm. She is very brave. Her mother collapsed; they think she died instantly. Gaia stayed with her, holding her hand until I got home that night. I had been working on a property. She was only three. We speak of Katerina a lot but rarely of the day she died. It was hard to get her to leave her mother when they needed to take her body. She didn't understand.' I tucked myself almost under him and wrapped my arms around his chest. His arms covered me; I was back in the safety of my big cosy blanket. I wished I hadn't asked for another sad story. I scanned his house, noting the stark difference between his and my mother's. You could fit her whole house into his living room.

'That poor girl.' We sat in silence for a while, just holding each other, propping each other up.

'What do you want to do today?' he asked, looking down at me, and then kissed the top of my head.

'I need distraction. Yesterday was much too real. The things that poor woman had been through. He fractured her cheekbone once and made her lie to the police and the hospital, making her say she was mugged.'

'That's dreadful.' His tone was cold, with only a hint of anger to it, but his eyes were full of fire. His reaction drew me even closer to him. I felt bad for not telling him before Nico. It wasn't as though I'd intended to see him, or tell him anything. When I needed support, Anton had been consistently there for me. I looked up at him and brushed my thumb lightly across his bottom lip and across his stubbled cheek. Even though there was no denying his good looks, that's not what drew me to him. It's not what made me ache. It was every fibre of his being. The words he said with just his vibrant eyes, the way his hands touched my skin. His fits of giggles and the way he looked at me. As though he would do anything for me. I felt alive with him no matter what we were doing. As though my blood had been replaced with electricity and I couldn't fight it. With each interaction my feelings for him were being pulled deeper. I was afraid if we did take it to the next level, I'd never be able to leave. But how could this possibly be my reality? It didn't feel real. But he was real – the feel of his flesh under my fingertips was real. I ran them over his long clavicle in amongst his lightly hairy chest. My mother's advice ran through my mind: *Do what makes you happy while you can.* I sat up and put my leg across his lap to face him. He was a picture of surprise, which made me laugh out loud. I felt so small in his embrace and nuzzled my face into his neck. Slowly he rubbed his hands along my spine and caught one of his fingers in my crochet dress.

'I think there's a hole in your dress,' he whispered into my ear, followed by a deep laugh that I felt through my thighs.

'What?' I whispered with mock surprise. 'You must have broken it!' I jokingly pulled a sad face and so did he.

'You'd best take it off if it's broken.' The corners of his mouth curled up into a smile as he carefully lifted the dress over my head.

My desire to hold him and never let go outweighed anything else in my mind. He lifted me to my feet with ease so I was standing in front of him. He lightly kissed my stomach, his thick eyelashes and brows tickling me. He stood up, took my hand and led me upstairs.

The only noise was the creaking of the wooden steps, and possibly my heart beating outside my chest. I followed him into the large master bedroom. I can't remember what I imagined it to be; either way, it wasn't what I thought. It was simply decorated with navy blue walls, white furniture and crisp virgin-white sheets.

'I can't stop thinking about you. I'm consumed by you,' he said, as he sat down on the end of the bed, creasing all of the perfectly laid sheets. He was still holding my hand and brought it to his lips. 'I want you. Not just now. I want you. I think you know.' He was studying my face as he spoke.

I did know. But I didn't know if I should admit it out loud. After everything I'd been through, everything the world had been through, I decided it was time to just forget. Time to live in the here and now of each moment. There was no past, no future, only him. Nothing else was guaranteed, nothing else was real. I held his face and kissed his bottom lip.

'Don't hurt me,' he whispered with a smile. He tried to make it playful but we both knew it was honest. The idea rang in my ears and sounded absurd. How could I hurt this sizeable man? Of course, I knew what he'd meant and I knew I could. I was equally likely to get hurt here and I didn't care any more. I had no power left for caring. My only requirement was him. I nuzzled his masculine scent, hard to describe, fresh but deep, intense. I carefully shuffled his top over his head.

'I wouldn't want to hurt you,' I said playfully, then lightly bit his bicep and glanced up at him. He laughed but looked a little surprised. I gently kissed the area and lightly teased his skin with my tongue as I eased up and kissed him. Like a vice, his hands became firm on the base of my back and hips, pulling me on top of him. He kissed me like we had been given a death sentence and these were our last moments. His hand was in my hair at the nape of my neck, and he very gently pulled to kiss my neck.

'Getting your own back, are you?' I laughed but if he had wanted to, he could crush me in an instant.

'Maybe,' he replied, but released his hold to sit me up and remove my top. Even though I was full of fresh pulses of nerves and excitement throbbing over my skin, I'd never felt so confident with a man. He sat up too and held me in his arms, with his head held between my breasts. I could almost hear him thinking. I didn't dare ask; I knew he was debating how far this should go and if we were right to invest in each other. I held his mind in my arms. I couldn't bear the volume of his silence and the comfort of his hold. My life had imploded enough. I started to gently move my hips to rouse his mind back into the moment. He was brought to my attention in an instant and there was no hiding it.

'How long has it been?' I breathed into his ear.

He made a growling hum noise that resonated in his chest.

'Too long.' He laughed off my question.

'Seriously.' I continued to motion back and forth gently.

'I broke it off with my last girlfriend before moving here, so, then.' His shoulders lifted shyly and fell with a small jolt. I took his face in my hands, scratching at his coarse stubble. I teased his mouth with my tongue and gently pushed him down between the pillows. I found my way down his long torso, studying him as I went. From the hairs on his chest to his clear-cut tan line just at his hip. I held him in my hands and watched him with each movement. Taking a man of his size and turning him into a quivering mess was, of course, very satisfying. But when you want to take care of them, hold them, make them feel the way you feel for them, it creates an intensity I'd never felt. I wanted him to be lost before I found him again, before I brought him back from the brink, with only a practical pause for contraception before I took him. I slid myself down the length of his body and we both shuddered in mutual delight. I took my time as we entangled ourselves into one delectable creation. After all our lust and connection it wasn't long before we couldn't take a second more and together our flesh exploded in sweat and rapture.

It's funny – I hadn't expected any of it to happen when or how it happened. Not after the day before. But somehow the emotional upheaval had just pushed me into his arms even harder. I realised how much I needed to hold his flesh in my hands and to hide in our extraordinary connection.

We lay next to each other, holding hands.

'I'm starving,' I said eventually, and turned to face him.

His hair was all ruffled, which looked even sexier than his normal, styled, look. His bed bounced as he giggled.

'I wasn't enough for you?' He gave an expression of faux upset, laughed harder and got out of bed. 'What do you want?'

'To stay here and look at you.' I wiggled down into the sheets so I was just peeping over the top of them.

'Sorry, Mou, that's not on the menu.' He left the room, to my immense disappointment.

The thought that I must ask what this "Mou" nonsense was about, floated through my mind. My eyelids were feeling heavy. It had been worse than I thought. I had fallen completely. Nothing could have prepared me for the intimacy we had shared, a level no words could truly describe. I had loved men before, of course, but this felt so different. Like we already knew each other, had done for years and not weeks. I could no longer hold my eyes open, and I peacefully fell asleep in our newly dirtied white sheets.

'Ta-da!' He burst through the door, startling me from my nap, then he was cursing in Greek, as far as I understood.

'Did I wake you?'

I took one look at him and burst out laughing. He was wearing a tiny makeshift apron around his waist, only just covering his manhood. He held a tray in one hand, perfectly posed.

'What are you doing?' I was curled up with laughter.

'I was being your man-slave again. I'm so sorry to wake you...' He cringed and crept in.

'No, you're perfect, come here.'

He had made a Greek salad with lots of feta and olives – my favourite.

'Why are we eating this up here when there's a perfectly good table downstairs?' I asked with a point of my fork.

'I didn't want you to feel as though you had to put your clothes back on. If we went downstairs you might have considered them.' His full lips curved into a wide smile, eyes brighter than ever.

It was funny – the beautiful tension and anticipation between us was still running high. Now we both knew what we could expect, there was only desire to repeat the excursion. It gave me pangs of guilt; I couldn't know if this could go anywhere or not. I couldn't even let myself think about Gaia. It was hard not to establish myself in their life while trying to explore the relationship.

'What time is it?' I asked. I hadn't the slightest clue.

He pointed to a large clock on the wall, which I hadn't even noticed.

'Twenty to two,' he smiled and I lightly pressed my palm into my forehead at not noticing the sizeable silver clock.

'We still have the whole day ahead of us. What time will Gaia be home?' I asked, but I was quite sure I knew the answer.

'She won't. Well, not tonight anyway. When are you seeing your mother again? I assume you will want to?'

As he spoke, I studied the contours of his face, his prominent straight nose, bone structure you could cut diamonds with and his fuzzy facial hair softening the masculine lines.

'Tomorrow,' I replied. 'I don't think I can stay. I don't have anything with me.'

'You're kidding,' he said, looking seriously disheartened.

'I am kidding. I brought a little bag just in case. Not that it's a big deal, it's not like I'm staying far away.' I smiled.

'Well, well, teasing me, huh?' Raising a bushy eyebrow in my direction, he put his plate down just to turn and pounce on me like a cat, making me scream with laughter.

'Do you know what?' he said while kissing my neck and pinning me to the bed.

'*What*?!' I erupted between giggles. He was still intentionally tickling me but now with his tongue on my neck and his hair on my chin.

'I feel you had your way with me, and now it's my turn.' His hand travelled along the length of my leg, tickling my abdomen on the way to my breast. He licked and nibbled his way across my body, making me squirm and wriggle at his will. Eventually, his mouth settled between my thighs with one arm wrapped around my waist, locking me to him – not that I wanted to be anywhere else. He knew what he was doing. I felt as though I broke under his touch, broke into grains of Greek sand and disappeared into the sheets. He gave me only seconds to pull myself back together before wrapping my legs about his waist while he held mine and lured me to him. He looked me in the eye the entire time, fingers entangled in the hair behind my ear while stroking my clavicle with his large thumb. He took his time. He built me up all over again and we watched each other surrender to the warmth of each other's touch.

After spending the whole day exploring one another, we decided to go back to Taste Me for dinner. The name felt incredibly apt given the events of the day. I had a little giggle to myself but didn't say anything to Anton. Clearly he was thinking the same thing as he indicated towards the signage and gave me an exaggerated wink and tap on the bottom. The childish comedy induced a sigh and a small laugh that I gave up unwillingly. We ordered cocktails on our way past the bar and sat down to watch another stunning Corfu sunset.

'So, who taught you how to be so good?' I quizzed with a grin and he burst into a booming laugh, making people turn to look in our direction.

'That's not what I thought you were going to say!' He kissed my hand over the table. 'I've only been with three women, so you could say one of them, but I don't think it works like that. Each experience is individual. None is the same. Sometimes you just connect with someone and your body responds to them.' His green eyes looked at me like loaded guns, with black eyelashes framing the barrels. How was this man so often right?

'*I agapi eine agapi, den exei exigisi.*' He spoke very slowly, but I still didn't understand him. He was gently rubbing my hand and looking at my face.

'What did you say?' I asked, with both a longing and a fear to know the answer.

He just smiled, kissed my hand again and shook his head. We drank cocktails, ate delicious food and enjoyed each other's

184

company. It had been a perfect day.

Chapter 22

I woke up early. I wanted to know my mother more and desperately wanted to help her. It was time she was enabled to strive for a normal life. She hadn't deserved what had happened to her. A mildly rebellious teen she may have been, but her life was dragged off the rails and I wanted to set it all straight – as straight as I could. I kissed Anton goodbye, got in my car and made my way to her home. I only stopped to pick up fresh flowers for her.

When I arrived outside the house, I thought I should remember to offer to repaint her door and window frames – the blue paint was peeling off all over. Everything was run down; it didn't matter – I'd help to sort it out. I knocked with confidence.

'You knocked! You realise this is Greece. Even when Adam was alive we didn't lock the door and he was the most paranoid person I know of. He was also the only person I knew much of, of course. So not a lot of competition.' She smiled at me.

I felt a little scandalised about her blasé joke, but I suppose it was her life; he was her normal for twenty-four years while he was alive – maybe not her choice, but all she knew. I smiled back at her anyway.

'I forgot myself and reverted to my English ways. Sorry about that.' I passed her the bunch of roses I'd managed to buy. My second gift for her. I wanted her to know she was wanted. 'These are for you. I hope you like them. Sorry it's not much. I don't know what sort of thing you like.' I felt myself go a little pink. Silly really, but I couldn't help it.

'That's incredibly kind of you.' I noticed the photo and frame had taken centre stage on the heavy sideboard. It was funny how, even in this very new parent-child dynamic, being a child was exactly how I felt very quickly and easily.

She had made a real effort; if I were to guess, she was wearing her Sunday best. An ice-blue round-neck linen dress. It made her look like a shapeless rectangle but it was still pretty on her slim frame. Based on the life she had lived, trying to be an androgynous rectangle may have made life easier perhaps. She was tiny, a little waif of a woman, pretty and endearing like a soft little bird. Her hair was neatly tied into a bun on her head, wrapped in a navy blue scrunchy. All the blues brought out her eyes, blue like Grandpapa's. I followed her into the kitchen.

'Would you help me with these, please? I thought we could eat a brunch in the fresh air. If you'd like?' she said, pointing at blue plates filled with pitta bread, tzatziki, honey feta and homemade fairy cakes.

'Sounds perfect.' Picking up a couple of plates, I made my way to the table outside.

We sat down together, ready to eat and share more information about our lives. But instead we sat quietly. Just trying desperately to get used to each other's company after the

187

tortuous conversations of our last meal together.

'I thought you might like to see some photos of Grandmama and Grandpapa a few years ago in Corfu,' I announced while scrolling through my Facebook page to find the right album. 'Here!' I passed her my phone with a gorgeous photo I'd taken of them both. Grandpapa with a beer in hand, thick chalk-grey hair swept to one side. Grandmama with a glass of white wine, with red-orange lipstick to match her floral top. They must have been late seventies in the photo. They both looked fabulous, vibrant, happy. They'd had my mother later on — Grandmama had been thirty-seven and Grandpapa had been thirty-nine when they had her. I remember my mama telling me she had been cursed with miscarriages, but it wasn't something she discussed with me much. She was only closed on the subject of all the children she had lost, which included my mother.

My mother studied the photo intently for a while before she brought herself to say anything.

'They look so happy. I have missed them terribly over the years. It's strange to think this was in Corfu. So close and yet so far.' My mother seemed so different to our first meeting. As though our time together was working to change her outlook on life – or perhaps her attitude? She definitely seemed more relaxed than ever before. Maybe the weight had been lifted and there was nothing between us, nothing holding us back.

'Do you have any photos of you when you were little?' She passed back my phone with wide eyes.

'Not many of me. I have posted a couple on socials in the past...' I started to scroll frantically, wanting to please her. 'Here! It's another holiday snap. We were in Crete. I had just found a crab shell and it quickly became my pride and joy – no idea why, but that's it there' —I prodded at my phone— 'there in my hand. I was a slightly odd child.' I laughed but she didn't.

She was looking at the photo with a glazed-over smile, staring, eyes unmoving.

'I'm so sorry I didn't get to see you grow up. What a cute little girl. I'm so grateful to see this, to see you as a child. How old were you there?'

'I think I'm about four or maybe five. I'm grateful to see you now! I'm not going to lie to you, I have found it hard, coming to terms with the reality of what happened. At least in my head you'd always been happy away from me. I'd never even considered the contrary to be true…' My words trailed off as I took a sip of water. I needed to turn the conversation to something more positive again. 'I was wondering if you would like to come with me to Corfu town this week?' I didn't want to look at her in case she said no. There was a long pause and I eventually had to look at her. Her face seemed different today; I think perhaps she was somehow as determined as me to make up for lost time.

'Let's just worry about enjoying today,' she said and passed me a cake.

Perhaps an outing was a bit of a push for someone who didn't have a normal capacity for socialising.

'These cakes are delicious. You know, you're likely the strongest person I know. To put up with everything he put you through. I'm proud that you're my mum,' I said, looking down at my cake, holding the tiny casing, desperately trying to keep all the crumbs from falling away. It was the first time I'd called her "Mum". I glanced across at her. She wasn't smiling. Far from it. Her eyes had misted over and were facing towards the tiny grave of my tiny brother.

'I'm ashamed of it all. That I couldn't be there for you. I feel endlessly guilty that I didn't tell my parents about your father when I had the chance. That I was too afraid to send a letter home. I was weak. I missed out on seeing my parents one last time because of my fear and shame, even when he had passed. I'm – I'm weak. I'm so sorry for that.' Her voice had become no more than a whisper, floating along like a butterfly, tickling my mind with her despair. A chill ran along my spine. Her words, her tone, her expressions were chilling.

'Don't be absurd,' I blurted with an awkward laugh. 'They'd understand. I understand!' I was doing my best to bring her back to me.

She snapped out of her little trance and looked right at me. 'I guess we'll never know. We'll never know a lot of things.' She shrugged and took the plates back to the house.

Perhaps I was pushing her a little too hard again. I stayed for an hour or two more, telling her stories of my childhood. Answering questions about how old I was when I took my first steps, had my first boyfriend, what I got in my GCSEs, where I studied my degree, my favourite food, childhood pets and friends.

'Did Adam have any good points? It's been hard finding out the type of man that fathered me.' I looked off towards the bottom of the garden, trying to avoid looking at my brother's tiny grave. It was a very small garden, but I narrowed my eyes as though I was looking into a far-off hopeful land.

'He was an intelligent man, relatively handsome. He could charm anyone he liked. He always had a good job because he had a good head for numbers and statistics. That's a lot of good points, I think.'

'I do like maths and statistics – that's pretty much half of my job.'

'You definitely get that from him. I always liked reading and history at school. I have one photo of us if you'd like to see it?' She had barely finished before I was interjecting with a "Please". I didn't know what I was looking for or what I might find, but either way I needed to look. She got up, and I was trotting by her heels like an obedient horse in dressage.

'He asked someone to take it – it's of both of us from before you were born. I think I would have been two or three months pregnant. He took me out for Italian food and, actually, I think he asked the waiter to take it.' She was scrabbling through the sideboard in the sitting room as she spoke. 'Here – here it is. That's us.'

I carefully took the photo as though it was a ticking bomb that might leave me scarred for life. I looked down at sixteen-year- old Lil and twenty-eight or maybe twenty- nine-year-old Adam. Other than incredibly dated clothing and hair, they looked to be a normal couple out on a date. I don't really know what I'd expected. They were sitting with bowls of spaghetti and glasses of wine. Sixteen. Adam looked so normal – handsome to plain in looks. His face wasn't memorable in any particular way. You wouldn't suspect who he was under his smile. He was quite fair – almost angelic in appearance. Round blue eyes and shaggy, not- quite-curtains-not-quite-mullet hair with a round face to match his eyes. My mother looked happy, vibrant and beautiful, with a timid smile in pink lipstick. Completely different to the woman I had met, although today she looked as though she was trying to have more of a confident air, just like that hopeful, pregnant sixteen-year-old. I hoped so. She deserved to have the chance to move on.

'You can keep it,' she said.

'Really?' I didn't really know if I wanted it. I wanted her, but not really him.

'Everyone should have at least one photo of their parents. Whoever they were.' She looked convinced in her decision. Perhaps she was right.

'Okay, well, thank you. I suppose I had better go, but I'll be back in a few days if that's okay?'

We walked out to the car for our goodbye. She held my hands and looked me up and down, taking me all in. I stood still for my appraisal, hoping I was measuring up accordingly. She then held me so tightly to her bony frame, I was afraid she might break. As she released me from her hold, she stroked my cheek and softly kissed the other one.

'I've always loved you and I always will. Appearing in my life has been a blessing I'll always be grateful for, back then and here today.' She spoke confidently — almost rehearsed — then went to stand in the doorway to wave me farewell.

I would be back in a couple of days. There was no rush. I had found her now and I wasn't about to let her go.

Chapter 23

I drove straight back to Anton, pleased with the success of my morning. He was waiting outside his door, leaning on the wall with his arms folded and one eyebrow raised. I opened my car door in line with him and shot an eyebrow right back at him.

'How long have you been standing there like that?' I said with a smirk.

He pulled his phone from his shorts pocket to check.

'About ten minutes. I took a guess from when I got your message.' Grinning, he stepped forwards, looking me up and down, his eyes hesitating at my feet. 'Do you own any sensible shoes?'

I felt mildly offended by the enquiry. I joined his gaze and inspected my pretty pink flip-flops.

'It depends on your definition of sensible...' I shot him a little grimace.

'Why am I not surprised?' He huffed sarcastically, thrusting his hands into the pockets of his shorts.

'I can walk in these. Look, they have an ankle strap.' I wiggled an ankle in his direction.

'Are you sure? I'd like to take you somewhere and it involves some walking.' He was eyeing me dubiously, pressing his mouth tightly shut in consideration.

'I'll be fine.' I insisted.

'Oh well,' he shrugged, 'you're only small. I can always throw you over my shoulder.' He started towards me as though he was going to lift me like a fireman.

Loudly, I objected to the whole thing.

'I'm not small and you're not to lift me!' I was laughing again. Always able to make me smile, Anton seemingly could do no wrong. It wasn't not that I needed him to save me – only that his presence gave me the strength to feel free to live again.

'Okay then, Melodie-Mou, have it your way.' He slipped his fingers between strands of my hair and kissed me.

We got into his car and I paid no attention to where we were. I just let him drive. We stopped near some bins in what looked like a lay-by.

'Beautiful…' I uttered sarcastically as I turned my nose up. The sun was roasting the contents into a vile mixture of rotten veg and animal faeces.

'You're welcome.' He bowed equally sarcastically. 'This way, my girl, between the bins and the bird carcasses.' He looked up from his bow and gave a little wink. Grabbing a picnic basket from the car, he then led me in between the trees. He had been right; it was a little bit heavy going in my flip-flops. I was determined not to admit it.

'Do you want a lift yet?' he teased.

'No, I'm fine, thank you. Look, a little lizard.' I pointed by way of distraction. I could tell he knew, from his sideways glance.

'Come on.' He stopped and crouched down. 'Hop on!

Seriously! A piggyback will be easier than watching you wince every time you stand on anything.' He indicated with his head as I hesitated.

I went for it. I slightly hitched up my skirt and pounced on for the ride through the trees and the brush.

'Don't worry, it's not far now anyway.'

It was another sweaty afternoon in Corfu, which was accentuated by having my body pressed against Anton's. He was carrying me and a basket while traipsing up a slight incline. I was pleased I'd hitched a ride, though. I had my arms around his neck and his hair in my face; it smelt faintly of exotic flowers. I was enjoying being so high up, bounding through the fruit trees, occasionally dodging a branch. I'd always thought I was tall but he was exceptional. If we had children, they could be really tall too.

'How tall was Katerina?'

'Maybe five foot five – why?'

'Just, Gaia doesn't seem to be exceptionally tall like you, although I guess there is still time.'

'I hope she doesn't end up as tall as me.'

With that I was back to daydreaming as I was jostled along. It was nice to relax and take it all in: the crunching of Anton's feet mixed with the buzz of insects – sounds that you could hide in – you could be audible and still not be heard amongst the busy mosaic of sound. I pressed my cheek into Anton's hair, soft and prickly all at once. At that moment I had an urge to say "I love you". I had been denying my feelings but at that second, surrounded by nature's noises, my mind quietly told me the truth. I didn't say it, of course. I pushed it to one side; I wasn't ready to believe in love.

'Here we are,' he said, as the sea came into view. There were large slabs of rock protruding into the undulating turquoise blanket known as the Mediterranean. We were quite high above, looking down on it all. Carefully, he put me down and walked me towards the shade of a tree. He revealed a blanket from his basket and placed it on the large, flat, grey surface. This was swiftly followed by champagne popping and spilling over the neatly placed blanket.

'Bloody typical. I guess romance isn't my forte.' He gave a deflated sigh and grabbed for a napkin.

'Don't be silly! This is all perfect. Plus, what's perfection without a wet bum?' I gave a sly look and grabbed his bottom hard, before choosing carefully where to sit. 'It'll be dry in no time on this hot rock anyway, so there's nothing to worry about.'

'You haven't said much about today. How was she?' he said, while pouring the champagne into elegant — albeit plastic — flutes. I took my bag from across my body and pulled out the photo I'd been given, taking one short glance at it before I passed it to him without saying a word.

'Well. That's got to be your mother.' I nodded. 'I take it that's him? That's Adam?'

'It is.'

'He looks so normal. How do you feel about seeing him?' He passed back the image and I carefully put it away.

'Okay. It's hard to believe all the things he did from that photo, though. He looks positively baby-faced!' I sipped my champagne a little harder than I should have in the heat of the afternoon. It was at that point in time a hornet decided to fly between us, making me instinctively swat my hand and resulting in throwing champagne all over my dress. 'What an idiot!' In trying to use the blanket to mop me up, Anton then managed to pull over his glass, soaking his shoe.

'What are you doing? I thought I was the clumsy one!'

Neither of us could help but laugh.

'I don't know! This isn't at all how I planned it.'

We laughed but between the heat of the day and our sticky mess the romance had fallen flat. We stayed a short while, watching the boats in the distance coming and going, dancing on the waves. In the end we finished what was left of the bottle of champagne, ate some olives then packed up the box to head back. Halfway to the car I decided to dismount from my piggyback and walk for myself.

'Is Gaia about? I wanted to chat to her about sensible shoes. It seems if I'm staying here I might be needing some... Ouch! Shit!' Right on cue something sharp dug into the toe I'd hurt at Angelokastro castle. 'Shit! Shit!'

Anton dropped the basket and helped me to a grassier patch between the trees. A small twig stuck into the wound, making it bleed again. 'I think Corfu hates me. Maybe that's a sign I shouldn't stay,' I said, without any irony, with fear that I only had a day or two left and I still didn't know what to do.

'As long as the people don't,' he smiled down at me. 'Let me look.' He studied it then kissed close to the wound. 'All better.' He absentmindedly rubbed my leg. He couldn't have known what he had done at first, but his touch stirred something up in us both. Suddenly my toe was no longer of first concern. I glanced around. Other than lizards and insects, we were quite alone. He leant forward to kiss me but instead he hesitated, giving a small smile so close to my face I could almost feel the hair from his chin.

'*Eise to panda gia mena*,' he said; it could have been a question. Slowly resting his head on my shoulder, for just a moment,

197

before I felt the light touch of his hand along my thigh. He ran his finger under my knicker line as he gave in and kissed me.

'What does that mean?' I pulled away but held his white t-shirt tightly in my fists, squeezing it around his chest.

'It means you should learn a little Greek.' He put on a stronger accent than he normally had and kissed my neck.

'No, really, what did you say? It's so unfair. It's a hard language.'

'Unfair?' he continued between the tiny kisses he was planting like seeds of desire and anguish. '*Gamoto*,' he growled. 'You're unfair. You fall into my life when I was perfectly good. Look what you've done. Come here,' he breathed and sat down next to me against a tree, pulling me on top of him. He brushed me down, cleaning off dried grass and leaves, then turned his attention back to his planting of kisses, now across my shoulder and arm. He held me tightly, both arms bound around me.

'Please tell me.' I didn't know why I wanted to know so badly; that's a lie – I did. I wanted it to be "stay" or "I love you". I was becoming increasingly frustrated. He looked up at me but didn't stop kissing; he punctuated each word with a fleeting kiss.

'You. Mean. Everything. To. Me.' Then one more kiss under my jawbone. 'Happy now?'

I was already bothered from the fever of the air. I wished I hadn't asked. It wasn't "I love you", but it was as close as it could be. I actually think it meant more to me than if he had said "I love you". I could feel myself falling into the lap of Corfu, not just his. I put my hands on his face, smoothing his brow with my thumbs, and looked closely at the colours and textures of his eyes; green with thin flecks of blue and turquoise. They reminded me of my opal ring.

'Happy,' I confirmed.

'*Eise poli omorfi*,' he said with a laugh in his throat. Then he kissed me, hard, before I could question him again. He ran his hands around the line of my waist, drawing me to him. In turn I ran my fingers along his neck and he slipped his hand beneath the soft cotton of my dress, thumb caressing my nipple, drawing its attention like a soldier on the march. I lifted my weight and unzipped him beneath me, finding his own confession of wanting between my fingers. I toyed with him, reliving the memory of a feeling, and the anticipation of having it again. He was moaning somewhere deep in his chest, as I slid the protection between us. With an agonising drop in my weight, I exhaled deeply in his ear, fingers at his hard shoulders. Together we swayed like the ships on the sea, until I was holding onto the tree behind him to ground myself before I was lost. He whispered to me in Greek – I wasn't sure if it was to tease me, taunt me, or because he just didn't want to be understood. Together we burst into flames and only the puddles of sweat were left to contain us.

We were both panting, he took my face in his hands and whispered, '*Eise poli omorfi*', again. I flattened my face into a frown, which triggered an eye-roll from him.

'You're so beautiful! But I definitely should've said you need to learn some Greek!'

We picked ourselves up from where I had fallen, and carefully walked back to the car.

With the cool air rushing over my face, I was glad of his convertible.

'You know,' I said, grasping his knee as we went along, 'I read once that in Ancient Greece, sex and sexuality was intrinsically linked to all of creation. That, even today, sex is central to Greek identity.' I squeezed his knee a little tighter. 'So, what do you say? True or false?'

'I can only speak for me, and remember, I'm only half Greek.'

'True, but your opinion is the one of most value.'

'*Efcharistó*. Well, I suppose in some wáy it is. Who you choose, and why you choose them, is a reflection on identity.'

I considered the consequences of his words.

'So why did you choose me?' I tried not to make my words sound needy as we pulled into his drive, my hair whipped across my face and into my mouth in a way that was reminiscent of the day we met. I tilted my head down to retrieve the hair while waiting for a cheesy response. He didn't answer. Instead, when I looked up, he was frowning. I looked at the house to see a young girl sitting on the doorstep.

'Who's that?' I looked from her to him, waiting for more information to come my way.

'That's one of Gaia's friends, Nefeli.' He was out of the car quickly with a calm tone, but his body was stretched to his full intimidating height. I don't know if it was intentional, but as he walked across the dirt driveway, small clouds were puffing up around him, making it look like he was a monster emerging from the ground. The girl looked young for her age but didn't seem too worried by Anton.

'*Yassou*, Eli.' That was all I picked up on as they went into Greek. He didn't introduce me or even acknowledge my presence. I went to my car and hovered, pretending to get something out of the boot. I shuffled about. I was trying to blend in but I was more like a potato trying to hide in the stones. Anton suddenly seemed very agitated and paced out a small circle like a caged bear. The girl had started to go pink and kept shrugging. Poor thing. I took this as my cue to butt in.

'What's going on?'

Anton's head snapped round at me as though I was an unknown factor he had forgotten all about.

'Gaia. She told me she was with Eli, but Eli is here as Gaia borrowed her mum's necklace and she wants it back.'

'Oh, that's not Eli's fault. Does she know where Gaia is?'

'Don't you think I'd be on my way there if she did?' he snapped.

'Do either of you have any idea?' I did. I knew. I didn't want to be the one to say if I didn't have to.

'See was at the beatz with...' My stomach was contracting as I knew what she might say through her heavy accent. She pushed little green glasses along the bridge of her nose and glanced between us nervously. '...with Finn. Not there now.'

Anton instantly went into a flurry of Greek.

'I take it you know who Finn is?' I asked Anton, even though I knew the answer. I didn't know whether to just tell him I knew about Finn too, or whether to lie. I didn't want to lie; but I didn't want to lose Gaia's trust.

'Yes. Eli, you can go home now. Please apologise to your mother.' He then slipped back into Greek and the girl got on her bike and hastily left.

'Don't be too harsh on her.'

'Eli? No. She knows it's aimed at Gaia,' he said.

'No, I meant Gaia.'

'What,' he growled. 'Finn is her ex-boyfriend. So, I thought. I didn't like the boy. He's a player – and older.' He was pacing a little, somehow managing to answer me while deep in his own thoughts.

'I know. What do we do?'

He stopped pacing to turn to me.

'We? No, I think you should go. I'll call you later.' Then his face changed; those green eyes had fire behind them. They turned dark and pointed.

I was holding my breath, trying not to even blink.

'You know... What do you know?' His voice was so low I wouldn't have been surprised if he'd made the ground shake.

'Gaia wanted advice, woman to woman. She made me promise not to tell you; please, please don't be mad. I was happy I was forming a bond with her.'

'And who said you could?' he snapped at me, and went back to his pacing.

'Well, you seemed bloody pleased about it at the time.'

He ruffled and pulled at his hair. Then he stopped and the dust in the air began to settle again.

'I've been doing this alone for ten years. I am glad she likes you, but she is thirteen. Don't keep things from me – you are the adult!'

'I know, but I didn't want to let her down either. Come on, I could be helpful. Maybe I could text her? Maybe she'd come home? Or you could go and look and I could stay here in case she comes back?' I didn't want to so easily be dismissed from their family — shown to the door as evidence of being an outsider in their little twosome.

His face softened, but only slightly. Perhaps he was reading my thoughts again, or at least my face.

'Okay, you can help. This isn't over, though. I don't like you hiding my daughter's secrets from me. You wait here. I'm going to get Gaia. He only lives a minute away.'

He jumped into his car and left. It was only then that it

202

dawned on me he hadn't opened the front door. Luckily, being Corfu, it had been left open. Eli obviously didn't think it right to wait inside. It was silent, bar the hum of the air conditioning. I walked the large circuit of the house, contemplating what my normal would look like if I lived here. Could I take on the role of stepmother to a teenage girl? Would we have more children? Was he going to forgive me for keeping Gaia's secrets? I traced my finger along the dining room table – would this be the table I'd be eating my meals at from now on?

Then a wall of sound smacked me out of my day-dreaming, making me whip round like a child who knows they're in the wrong. It was a wall of Greek at first and I'm pretty sure they had forgotten I was there — then suddenly there was something I could understand:

'Gaia, you're a child. If I say you're not seeing him, you don't see him! That's it!'

'You cannot tell me what to do! This is – this is sexist!' She added something in Greek.

'You can't talk to me like that. You're grounded.'

'It's not like you'd be here to even notice!' Her hands were on her hips and I could see she was wearing makeup, lashings of mascara, a bit like mine. I hadn't seen her wear anything like that before. She had a crop top and shorts on; she seemed so exposed. I think what happened to my mother had put us all on edge.

'Don't be ridiculous! I can be sure you are home all summer if needed.'

'No you can't! You're always off with your new girlfriend!'

Suddenly I was being pointed at and they were both looking in my direction.

'Hi, Gaia, how are you?' I sounded ludicrous and small in

amongst their shouting and flamboyant arm-waving. Silence hit; Anton pulled his forehead tighter together into creases I'd never have imagined were possible, but Gaia softened a little.

'Good, thank you. Apart from Dad only treating me like an adult when he wants to have sex with you. How are you?' How she hit softness with cutting sarcasms and truth so painfully was beyond me. Only a girl with fire in her belly can get that combination right. At this Anton seemed to grow a foot taller and his eyebrows hit the roof. The problem was she had made both of us blush and flustered and she damn well knew it.

'I'm okay, thank you. Sorry I had to tell your dad about our conversation,' I muttered, shifting my weight from one hip to the other as though my legs were getting ready to run.

'You spiteful little girl,' he growled at her. Her eyes and cheeks were washed with pink and a tear fell from her lower lash straight to the floor. Then her hands were off her hips and punching down by her sides.

'Go to your room,' he said quietly, and she did just that.

We stood still, left in the thick smog of the argument. Angry breaths huffed and puffed from Ant's chest; I didn't want to be the first to speak.

'I think you should go. I need to look after my daughter.' His face was a vibrant purple-red and for the first time I was happy to leave. I skulked past him without even a kiss.

I drove back to my Corfu home feeling utterly confused and abandoned. I didn't feel welcome in their life and it left me with a thousand questions. Later that evening I got a message just saying "sorry". I didn't reply. I couldn't think of any words to say.

Chapter 24

I was up early to see my mother again. I was quite excited to tell her about my love drama. Even though she perhaps didn't have conventional life experiences, I wanted her opinion on it all. With or without a frame of reference. I stopped to buy some sweet treats to take with me to gossip over.

I arrived at her door itching to see her. She knew I was coming, and it was Corfu, so I knocked and walked in simultaneously, calling out for her as I went.

My eyes caught sight of her sitting in her chair. At first, I thought she was asleep. She was tightly wrapped in a thin, pale blue dressing gown, which didn't quite cover her knees, and her hair was perfectly placed around her shoulders.

Only, her eyes were wide open.

And so was her mouth, and her head rested heavily on the back of the chair.

Dropping the cakes I was carrying, I took two strides to be next to her. I touched her face, but even in the heat of the room she was cold. Tears clouded my vision as I begged her to wake up, even though I knew that she wasn't really there.

I could hardly breathe. Each breath was shorter and sharper than the last. I clutched my mother's left hand in both of mine. I kept asking myself: why hadn't I held her tighter or stayed longer the last time I'd been with her? I shouldn't have left her. I should have taken her with me. Why had I left so bloody early? Eventually, amongst the whirl of questions, I managed to take one large breath to save myself from suffocating in my sorrow.

All of a sudden, my freshly deranged mind took me to Gaia. At only three years old, she had had to grow up. She had watched her mother pass, and had held her cold hand. Neither one of us could have predicted or understood these sudden losses. My mother's eyes were still wide open. Reaching up, I tried to shut them, only for them to spring back open again. It wasn't what I'd expected – stupid to think it would be like something in a film. I wondered if that had happened with Gaia too, and what a three-year-old would have thought? Perhaps she'd have thought it was a game. I pressed my mother's lids closed and held them there until they stayed closed. Focusing on Gaia and closing my mother's eyes had distracted me just enough to begin to process what was in front of me and what I needed to do.

Still kneeling by her side, and holding her hand, I took my phone from my pocket with the other. My hands were shaking as I dialled 112. Thank God the lady on the line spoke English, but as I described the scene to her, it was hard to hold back from vomiting.

My chest was still trembling from crying as I waited for the police and the ambulance to arrive, and my eyes were full of mascara flakes. I cleared them a little with my fingertips, and that's when I noticed a little notebook on the floor by

206

my mother's bare foot. I picked it up, while still holding my mother's hand, much like Gaia had with her mother. I was reluctant to let go, yet I couldn't help but open the little yellow book. It was her diary. There weren't very many entries so I quickly found her final one:

I am so looking forward to seeing Melodie again. Her beautiful face reminds me of Mum. I wish I had been able to see her and Dad at least once more. I need to tell Melodie the real reason I couldn't leave the island so easily. Honestly, I am dreading it. She has been so understanding so far about what I went through. What Adam put me through, I should say. I hope she won't think I'm mad when I tell her what I've found so far. Maybe I am.

I'm finding the headaches unbearable at times. I can feel the pressure of it now. I've been lucky not to have anything too dreadful when Melodie's been visiting. That is something I'm very grateful for. I'll have to tell her about the tumour at some point, though. I don't want to spoil it all before I really must. I wish I could have protected her against it all. I wish I could have protected the

That's where the diary entry ended – in mid-sentence. I read it back four or five times. First quickly, then more slowly as I took it in. A tumour? What sort? Where? Why hadn't she told me at the start?

There was a knock at the door before I was able to spiral again. Reflexively, I squirrelled the book into one of the pockets on the front of my dress, and opened the door to two young policemen. More people arrived and shuffled around her, around me. In broken English I eventually found out from one of the medics that she had known about her brain tumour for six months. Before they took her away from me, they let me have her necklace. I placed one small kiss on the scar on her eyebrow.

'No more pain, Mum. I love you.'

When I eventually got into my car, I felt the little diary in the pocket of my dress. I'd forgotten all about it. I carefully placed it on the seat beside me and drove back slowly – to the discontent of many other road users. I didn't care. My mind was full of questions, with no one left to answer them. I had had her for a matter of days and I hadn't used them wisely. I could've asked her about her childhood with Mama and Papa more. I could have focused on positivity. But I didn't. The morbid part of me had to pick at wounds and know what my father had been like. What he had done. Why? It was another hopeless question. Nothing could be done and nothing could be changed.

When I arrived back at the Airbnb, I didn't go in. I walked to the sea. I walked in without removing my yellow cotton dress. Just as I had my first night. With a heart filled with more loss and sorrow, I took myself under the calm waves. This time I chose to come back – I wasn't frightened by a fish. The past month had changed me. I had a new respect for the life my mum had given me and what she had protected me from. It had cost her her own life one way or another. I may have felt lost and confused again, but at least I didn't want to disappear for good.

It was evening by then and there were some people about. They must have thought I was crazy. I trudged back along the beach to the house, with mascara-covered cheeks and more aware than usual of how much sand had stuck to my feet. My phone was ringing, but I didn't look at it. I knew it was Anton, but my heart had closed. My whole body needed to shut down.

I sat at the breakfast bar shaking, teeth chattering like a rattlesnake's tail. She was gone. I kept saying those words over and over again in my mind. She was gone. What was I meant to do next? A part of me had thought I could live happily ever after on Corfu – a neat little package that included gaining a husband, a daughter and a mother. She was gone. I couldn't save her. I couldn't help her. She was gone.

I opened the little diary, but I couldn't keep my hand still enough to read. As I tried to look at it, my phone rang again: Anton. I considered answering this time. To have him hold me and warm me, and thaw through the cold and dread lingering over me. I felt as though I didn't deserve it, didn't deserve him. Or perhaps I was just frightened – frightened he was calling to tell me the dream was completely over. I went upstairs and got in the bath. I sat in it crying for an eternity. A whole eternity.

My phone buzzed again, this time a message from Maria:

Hey! How's your stay? Let's meet up? x

I replied:

I can come to Vicky's tomorrow morning. I'm leaving tomorrow night. x

Maria:

Okay, see you around 9? x

I had made my decision. I would leave. The plane was scheduled to depart the next night. I couldn't bring myself to see Anton and I knew if I stayed for even another week,

I would have given in to my desire to be held by him. If he even wanted to hold me. Leaving the next day would be better for everyone. I stepped out of my bath of tears and started to pack.

Slowly I made it downstairs and sat on the sofa, just staring at the wall. A knock on the door startled me out of my trance. I was sure it was Anton and I didn't know whether to just shout 'Go away'… Then Nico waltzed in.

'Sorry. I could see you in the window.' He stopped as he looked at me properly. His expression went from smiling Jack the Lad to concerned little boy. He rushed to sit by my side.

'What are you doing here?' I was bewildered.

'I don't have your number.'

'Okay.' I paused, waiting for more information, but it didn't arrive. 'So what are you doing here?'

'I like you. So here I am.' I was astounded. He sounded genuine too. 'You have been crying. What is wrong?' I looked into his boyish face. He didn't look all that much older than Gaia to me. No wonder she liked him. He definitely had a cool, teen band member vibe, which I could imagine worked on many girls of all ages.

'I found my mother, whom I hadn't seen since I was a few days old, only for her to die of a brain tumour.' I slowly turned my face away from him, giving him a chance to absorb my words.

'Tumour?' he asked.

I guess it's not a commonly used word when learning a language. 'She's dead,' I snapped. 'It killed her. It grew in her brain and it killed her.'

'I do not know what to say. You need a drink.' He jumped up and helped himself to whatever he liked in the kitchen.

Finding the ouzo, ice and short tumblers, he came back to my side.

'Why are you really here?' I couldn't believe it was a genuine house call.

'I told you. I have no reason to lie. If I want something, I get it. I think I made it clear I like you.' He smiled at me while thrusting his hand into his pocket. He pulled out a cigarette packet. 'These were meant for after.' He winked and poked his sharp little elbow at me.

'You silly sod,' I said with a frown, 'you can't smoke that in here!'

He just shrugged and cupped his hand round to light the thing anyway. Then he was off looking for an ashtray. 'So… what happened?' His wide eyes waiting for answers.

In some strange way it was nice to have him there. He might have had an agenda, but I didn't. I could just talk; it didn't matter much what I said. I told him what I'd arrived to and about the diary. I passed it to him to read. He waved it at me and asked me to read it out. Sharing the information with someone else was managing two things: the first was making it real all over again, but the second was to make me confront it. Which wasn't a bad thing.

'Fuck. I'm sorry, Melodie.' It was weird of him to call me by my real name. Nico put his arm around me and squeezed. 'Sounds like you made her happy.'

We sat like this for a short time while he smoked and I drank. It wasn't long before I was slurring and yawning.

'You sleep. I do not think you should be alone. I stay. I stay in the guest bed, yes?'

I was just pleased he hadn't tried to suggest sleeping in my room, so I quickly agreed and was asleep before my head hit my pillow.

Throughout the night I would hear the buzz of my phone, like a lonely bee hard at work. Sometimes I would look, sometimes I wouldn't. They were all him. All Anton. I couldn't deal with any of it. Most were messages demanding I let him know if I was all right. I couldn't sleep, not properly. As I fell in and out of dreamy consciousness everything fused together. One moment in the warmth of Anton's arms, then the icy fingers of my mother, calling me to help her. Eventually I got up. It was very early in the morning, maybe around three. I couldn't look at my phone again. At some point during my dreams, I had thrown it on the floor. I decided to go out into the warm air of the night. I crept past Nico's door and quietly down the stairs without putting on any lights. I opened the front door only to fall back onto my bottom. Anton was sitting there. He fell backwards through the doorway, knocking me flying. I didn't manage to save myself at all well. Most of the force of the fall scraped my hands and wrists as well as my bottom. After my blood-curdling scream, I was shouting.

'Why again? What are you doing here? Where is Gaia? And why do you always loiter in my doorway?'

He rolled over and helped me to my feet.

'Because I care about you! Clearly you don't feel the same with me! You don't care that I'm sat at home worrying about you. Not knowing if you're all right, or what's happening to you! I took Gaia to her grandparents earlier in the day to keep her from seeing that Finn until I know what to do with her.' His size was intimidating when he was upset. I wasn't afraid, but I did feel rather small and guilty. For the second time in twenty- four hours, I was putting myself in Gaia's shoes with a new- found respect. He had started waving his hands all about and was talking to himself in Greek. Then he looked at me with eyes glowing under a fierce frown. He turned and walked outside, leaving me standing alone.

Nico came rushing down the stairs with hair spray in his hand by way of a weapon.

'What the fuck?' he yelled at me.

'Nothing, nothing. Go back to bed.' I waved dismissively, wishing he hadn't been there at all. I walked across the room to the breakfast bar. Nico was still hovering on the stairs in his pants, bewildered, with hair like a caveman. I didn't have a moment more to think before the door nearly flew off its hinges and Anton almost forgot to duck when walking in, making me wince at his almost-pain. How he was creating so much commotion all by himself I had no idea. I just sat, stunned. Nico stood stunned. Both saying nothing, doing nothing. Anton was still fully animated and talking away at me in Greek. Too fast for me to take anything in at all. His arms were as mesmerising as wiper blades. He stopped, then stormed towards me and kissed me, almost knocking me off my chair.

'What have you done to me?' he said quietly, as he held my face. He kissed me on the forehead, hesitated and turned around, suddenly catching sight of Nico. He did a double take between us. I read his mind and started frantically shaking my head.

'Don't be bloody ridiculous,' I said. 'You know me and that's not me!'

'Do I?' His tone cut through me like a blade of ice. He turned and walked away, not giving Nico another glance. I couldn't hold in my desire to be held by him any longer. I wanted to fix it. I sprinted out of the door but it was too late. He had already pulled away. Perhaps it would be down to fate. He was either a good driver, regularly checking his mirrors, or he wasn't. I had to accept it either way. He didn't look back and see me. Or, if he did, he chose to carry on. I couldn't blame him either way. Hesitantly I walked back into the house. Nico was sitting on the stairs, already with a lit cigarette hanging out of his mouth.

'I think he likes you,' he laughed.

Pushing past him, I went to my room and cried for an eternity once more.

Chapter 25

I sat at Vicky's bar waiting for Maria. I was there early and I'd already had two shots of ouzo. I could now that I'd got rid of my hire car. Maria floated between the chairs and arrived at my table.

'Drinking already?' She clicked her tongue and shook her head. I just nodded. She ordered two orange juices and gave her father a peck on the cheek across the bar. She brought the juices back with her and handed one of them to me. 'You look like shit. You shouldn't be drinking so early. Drink this.' She lifted the heavy square chair before placing it where she wanted it.

'Yes, well. I found my mother lived here on the island. I met her. She then promptly died, and I found her then too. Oh, and I fell in love and pushed him away, partly with the help of bloody Nico – no, I didn't have sex with Nico... I'm unsurprised by my appearance. I spent most of yesterday crying, then Nico got me drunk. I probably do need this.' I picked up the juice with a 'cheers' gesture. 'I'm likely dehydrated from my leaky eyeballs.' I laughed at my own statement then drank the sharp, fresh juice. Maria was just sitting looking at me.

'Bullshit,' she said, and pressed her fingers to her lips.

'No, it's not.'

'That's all insane! No wonder I hadn't heard from you. I thought you were just annoyed at me.' She blushed a little.

'Well, I wasn't best pleased with your poor matchmaking skills, I have to say. But no, I've been quite busy.' I dismissed my upheaval with a shrug and underplayed everything that was in my head.

'I want to know more, or to ask a question, but I don't know where to begin...' She trailed off and rubbed her pretty, round face.

'It's okay. I'm only really here to say goodbye.' I took a sip of my juice.

'Who is he? The man. And what did Nico do?' she quizzed, blue eyes darting with anticipation.

'His name is Anton Greenwood.'

'I know Anton! He's hard not to notice, let's be honest. Especially when you're as short as me. Blimey, he is gorgeous and seems like a genuinely nice bloke.'

'He is,' I had to agree. 'In fact, he's bloody perfect.' I paused. 'I have never had sex in Corfu.' I then took a sip of my drink.

She gasped and squealed, making other customers turn and look. Rocking back into her chair, she clapped her hands. She never minded people looking. 'I'm impressed! I've never known him to date anyone. He always gets attention, but I've never known him to act on it. He always puts his daughter above everything.'

Her words cut through me. In my heart I knew I couldn't fit in. The problem was that each interaction just seemed to be

216

pointlessly reaffirming the bond that had been created.

'Don't tell me, he calls you Melo-Mou and whispers *t'amo*.' She clasped her hands together by her face and fluttered her lashes.

'That's not even Greek,' I sneered.

'Ha! I know. It was a joke!' She poked her tongue out at me.

But he did call me "Mou", all the time. I was flustered and spluttered my words.

'Why, what does that mean? "Mou"?'

'"Mou"? It means "mine". It's a term of endearment. I was just kidding, girl.' She wasn't kidding; she just didn't know it. The words jumbled up in my head.

'Yes, well, I guess he made an exception with me and then changed his mind. In part because when he turned up at my house last night, Nico was there. Nothing happened! Before you start! He came over because – well, he wanted something to happen, I guess, but he ended up being a shoulder to cry on. Nothing else.'

'That's some bad timing, girl.'

'Yes.' I couldn't take more going over things. I needed to be alone. 'Well, I'd best be off. Thanks for the drink.' I started to stand, struggling against the weight of the chair.

'Wait – you haven't told me what happened with your mum. That sounds dreadful!' she exclaimed, and stood with me.

'It was. But I'd like to pop up to the church before I go, and with this big suitcase it's going to take me ages.' I indicated my huge suitcase, for which I'd paid extra to bring on the flight. She offered to come with me, but I declined. I kissed her on the cheek and started my arduous march up the hill.

The words "mine" and "mou" kept rolling around in my empty skull. He said I was his; I wanted to be his. My mind was rattling as much as my jiggling suitcase. I was sweating and puffing from pushing it along. At least it had four wheels, which I was very glad of. When I made it to the church, I was mildly disappointed not to have come across Anton going in and out of places. Perhaps he was in Sidari. I set my suitcase just outside and made my way in. I sat quietly, absorbing the smoky, waxy atmosphere and the vibrant images. Last time I had sat there I was alone, and it wasn't my fault. Now I was alone and I felt wholly to blame. My mum had been taken from me for a second time, and I felt too emotionally damaged to include Anton and Gaia now. I didn't want to hurt them. I said a little prayer for them all. May they forgive me. He had asked me not to hurt him – I think perhaps he knew I would. It wasn't all me, though. He had pushed me away too, I told myself. I welled up again just at the idea of being encompassed in his arms one more time. We had had our one perfect day. It was more than I deserved. It had only been days since I was sitting in this very spot. It felt like a year. I was a changed woman. It dawned on me that I'd reverted to some sort of unruly teenager. I hadn't noticed it, but sitting in that church it hit me. The anger at losing my grandparents had kick- started a tantrum that coming back to Corfu had encouraged. I'd enjoyed being babied by Anton much too much. It had just been so nice to be cared for again. Then finding my mum had just made it all so much worse; how could I not feel like a child again? I'd been so bloody stupid. It was no wonder it hadn't worked out. I had even been drinking like an irresponsible teen and had the headache to prove it.

The whole time I sat there, the eye painted at the top point of the church watched me, looked down on me, judged me. I couldn't blame its judgy look; I deserved it for being such a child. I got up and lit a candle in memory of my mum. She hadn't deserved the life she had been dealt. I walked out into the cleansing rays of sunshine and decided to go to Fantasea for lunch before getting my cab to the airport.

More beautiful views. Looking across the bay gave me the escape that I required. Unfortunately, the calm was hollow and lonely, but a calm mind was welcome over a busy one. I had a farewell Greek salad and wondered why food was so emotive. I was looking at my phone. I hadn't taken many pictures on my trip. But the waiter at Taste Me had insisted on taking some of us together. We looked so happy. As I skimmed, I stopped on my mum's face. She had once told me to "do what makes you happy while you can"; she was likely thinking about her tumour. I shouldn't have let Anton leave. He made me happy. Fate let him drive away from me and I knew I didn't deserve such a kind and passionate man. That's when I saw him. He saw me in the same moment. My blood stopped in my veins and his emerald eyes cut through me. He turned to walk away.

'Wait!' I was screaming, knocking my legs into the table as I stood, leaving me hopping around rubbing my thighs as I danced towards him. 'Please wait!' Luckily the restaurant wasn't too busy, but the people who were there were getting quite the show. He didn't stop. He didn't look back. He just got into his van and left. I sat back down, feeling utterly foolish for thinking he could ever forgive me. Firstly, for ignoring him, secondly for the Nico mix-up.

As the taxi took me through the beautiful views of Corfu, I was relieved to be leaving it all behind. The weeks I'd spent there had been exhausting. I almost felt as though I needed a holiday to get over my holiday. I got to the airport, squeaky stilettos and mask ready for the journey. The journey to take me back to my two empty homes.

It had been just over a month since leaving Corfu. Cambridge had seen a lot of dry weather but that day it had rained. Heavy at first, then a light drizzle that left the air smelling of steamed grass and tarmac. I had managed to get a lot done since being back, helped by keeping a sober head. Single-handedly I had emptied Mama and Papa's house and put it on the market. I didn't think about it too much. I didn't think about anything too much. When I wasn't working, I had been there, filling boxes. Some to bin, some to keep and some to ponder over for hours. One of the days I had sat holding a half-full perfume bottle of Mama's, dwelling on its muddle of peonies and white musk. In the end I kept it. Every time I went near it, I felt like she was coming in for a hug.

My next project would be to decide what to do with my mum's house in Corfu. I'd paid a company to box her things and send them over in the coming weeks, but I still didn't know what to do with the house itself. Finding her and losing her so quickly felt like having a punctured lung. The only positive was the decision to mend my ways, as best I could. I was working more and gaining more from it and I had accepted a date with a man from an Instagram account I had been working on. My life had to be lived.

I was at Mama's and Papa's, moving the last few items into the clean white hire van. It was permeated with pine freshness – nothing like Anton's coffee and air con. I was muttering and swearing under my breath, trying to navigate a long bar speaker out of the front door. My leg was outstretched as I tried to push the door open so that I could escape without damaging the speaker or scraping a wall. I needed to move quickly as the rain had picked up its step. The van door had blown shut and I was trying to carefully prise it open with the end of the speaker.

'Do you need a hand with that?' The voice made me release a high-pitched gasp as I sharply turned, momentarily making the speaker into a jousting lance. I only just missed him. Anton.

'How on earth did you find me?' I'm not sure that's what I had meant to say. It came out all in a fluster, almost aggressively, barked out like a startled puppy. I was still aiming the speaker at his abdomen. I couldn't believe it; I'd avoided thinking about him directly. He would appear most nights in my dreams, and every morning that was where I would leave him. Then there he was.

'Can I come in?' He was wet, the tanned flesh of his forearms covered in goosebumps. His pale blue t-shirt clung to his body, showing his muscular frame, making my chest tighten at the memory of everything I'd tried so hard to forget.

'I guess so.'

He silently helped to place the speaker into the van and followed me into the house. 'Sorry, there's nothing to sit on. I've just finished clearing the place out.' His face had been very blank, even when I nearly speared him. His eyes were sunk below his brows and the little line between them had been there the whole time. I felt a little bit like my legs had become slinkies, wobbling about beneath me.

'What's going on? Why are you here?' I pursed my lips and folded my arms.

'Is there somewhere warmer we could talk?' he said through a tense jaw. His whole body was tense, in fact, with random shivers as his big hands clasped his own biceps for warmth.

221

I looked around, searching for an answer. It was all blank magnolia walls, with faded outlines where furniture had once lived.

'I know – go upstairs to the bathroom. It's on the left. I'll meet you there.' There was a hand towel I had left in the downstairs bathroom; it was all I could think of. When I walked in, he was wringing out his top into the roll-top bath. He looked down at me, letting me have the smallest of half-smiles. I gripped the yellow towel close to my body, a little rough and not all that dry itself.

'The quickest way to get warm is to have a shower. It's electric, so instant heat.' I pointed the towel to the corner of the room. My grandparents had had a level access shower fitted behind a ceiling-to-floor pane of glass. It wasn't exactly a wet room, but one end wasn't far off.

'Thank you,' he said and his face relaxed, the frown line lifting at last. His fingers moved to the zip of his jeans. I spluttered and turned to look at the smooth white tiles on the wall, sadly reminiscent of his sheets. Unable to stand the resemblance, I squeezed my eyes tightly shut and pressed the towel almost under my chin, inhaling its damp soapy scent. I could feel my flesh glow under my paint-stained denim shirt.

'Can you please tell me why you are here?'

He turned the shower on and didn't answer. I turned my head slightly to try to gauge if he had even heard me.

'Anton?' I called over the crashing of the water. He ignored me again. My fingers dug into the poor little towel. I clicked the towel rack on and placed the rough yellow fabric carefully over it. I then stood gripping it before turning to face him. I could see he was leaning his forearms on the shower wall, with his head bowed beneath them. Just leaning, letting the water create pathways over every muscle, between every hair. I twisted at my ring; round and round it went, like my mind, desperate to know what was going on.

'Please, Anton, I'm starting to really worry,' I called out to him again, fingers now scrubbing my forehead. He turned off the shower and stepped out in front of me. His wet body called to me. I managed to maintain his eye contact as I took in a juddered breath, pulled the towel off the rack and threw the little rectangle at him.

'Please – talk to me. This isn't fair.'

Patting at his face, then his hairy legs. He didn't shy away, he didn't hide from me.

'I'm sorry,' he started, at last, 'I'm sorry for everything.' His voice trailed and his eyes were on my feet. The thick black lashes framing his eyes made them almost look closed. The yellow towel balanced about his middle, his hand pressing to him.

'What do you mean?' I nodded towards the towel rack and we sat down in front of it.

'I bumped into Maria a couple of weeks ago. She mentioned how awful it was, what happened to your mother. I had no idea. I hadn't been to Agios Stefanos for a while.' He rubbed at his stubbly chin. I noticed he wasn't wearing his wedding ring any more. 'I also spoke to Gaia about it. She has more idea than me about losing a parent, and losing one in a – you know – a hard way. That sounded stupid.' He muttered in Greek and crossed himself; he looked to the ceiling but when he looked back at me, I was smiling; then he did too. 'She told me not to be too hard on you. That I couldn't imagine what you were feeling. She turned fourteen last week, Gaia.'

'I know. I text her.'

223

'What?'

'We both know she doesn't tell you everything. Clearly she doesn't tell me everything either or I'd be wearing more makeup.'

His chest gave a low vibration in an almost-laugh, then he gently touched my cheek with his thumb. 'She's right, of course. Maria also said you had had your mother's body sent back and that the funeral was next week. I was hoping I could be with you?'

I gently tugged on my necklace. It was my mum's, a beautiful green-blue opal, just like my ring.

'I know how I feel about you. It hasn't changed. I should have spoken to you then. I've been one thing for so long, a "father", nothing more. I'm used to being told what's going on or, so I thought, being the one in charge, being the carer. Alone, no help. Having Gaia ignore me and then you – I didn't handle it well. Uncertainty was too much for me. Plus, Nico in his pants – Maria explained that too.' We had started to hold hands as he spoke. I'm not sure at what point it happened, at what point his fingers crawled into mine, or maybe mine into his.

'It's funny – I'm the opposite. Losing my grandparents had made me act like a petulant child. Even before that, living alone for so long, not having anyone but my parents to answer to, and even then, as a grown woman, I obviously didn't tell them everything. I'm used to processing things alone. I wanted so desperately to talk to you, for you to hold me and make me feel better, but – well, firstly I needed to sort myself out, find me again. And, honestly, I was afraid of dragging you down or losing you – it was just easier to push you away. Or let you push me away from Gaia. I just wanted to protect you and her from all the negativity I felt.' Watching his face as I spoke, he couldn't stop himself smiling at the mention of Gaia.

'The fact you're worrying about how you might affect my daughter, says you're a good person. One we would cherish in our life. Gaia has said she misses the way I smile when I say your name. We can't have these misunderstandings. I want you. I don't want to be without you again. Having someone I love taken away from me again made me feel like a shadow. It was, in many ways, worse than when my wife died.'

'Love?' My cheekbones sat up on my face as I watched his thumb lightly rub the back of my hand.

'*I agapi eine agapi, den exei exigisi.*' He had said this to me once before; he repeated it again, quietly and slowly as he brought me into his arms to lie next to him across the cold tiles. 'Love is just love,' he repeated in English, 'it can never be explained.'

A note from the author...

Thank you for reading The Little Blue Door, the first in a trilogy of books following Melodie's story. I wrote this novel during the 2020 lockdown after having my second child. I've always been one to create my own version of freedom and this book was the ultimate way to do that during the first wave of the pandemic. My brain needed Corfu.

I love to read what you think about my work. So please remember to review (reviews change lives - trust me) and come and have a chat with me on my social pages too. **Instagram & Facebook: @FrancescaCatlowOfficial Twitter & TikTok: @FrancescaCatlow**

Before I sign off, I'd like to say an extra special thank you to my whole family, but in particular my mum. She has read this book more than me, I'm sure! The Little Blue Door trilogy wouldn't have happened without her.

Please Remember:

If you are a victim of domestic abuse, please ask for help. There are lots of charities you can contact. Here is a link to the

UK charity 'Refuge' that helps victims of domestic violence: https://www.refuge.org.uk/

Francesca x

A note from the author...

Thank you for reading *The Little Blue Door*...

CPSIA information can be obtained
at www.ICGtesting.com
Printed in the USA
BVHW070200050523
663650BV00019B/275